WITCH'S TAIL

THE SPELLWOOD WITCHES, BOOK 1

MELANIE SNOW

Spirit Paw Press, LLC

CONTENTS

The Spellwood Witches Series

Witch's Tail

Fish and Blame ~ A Free Novella

Howl Play

Tail of a Feather

Impawsible Mischief

Pawtrayal

Witch's Tail

The Spellwood Witches, Book 1

ISBN: 978-1-7324375-6-2

ASIN: B08H5TY2YC

(Spirit Paw Press, LLC, Concord, NH 03303)

www.wendyvandepoll.com/melanie-snow

Thank You

Download Your Free Gift

A Welcome to Witchland Map

Thank you for purchasing *Witch's Tail, The Spellwood Witches, Book 1*. To show my appreciation and because of a popular request from my readers
I am offering a:

Free Novella ~ Fish and Blame

https://wendyvandepoll.com/melaniesnowfishandblame

Lativia Spellwood sat on her ghostly throne of branches on the summit of Mount Katribus, with many other ghosts swarming around her reminiscing about life and drinking wine. The ghosts of Witchland residents always came to this clearing after they died to stay near Lativia for guidance and to wait until they were ready to pass on to the afterlife. Lativia had been dead for hundreds of years but had still not passed on, for her work oversee Witchland and its forest was not yet done. One day, it would be, and she was beginning to welcome that time, for she was growing very tired.

A tiny troop of Leekin faeries moved about the arms and legs of Lativia's throne, placing flowers into the holes between the woven boughs. They did that every day, as a way to honor her as Queen of the Forest.

Lativia sipped from a goblet of ghost wine, enjoying the blue fire as it spread down her throat, engulfing her in tingly warmth. Being a ghost was always cold; the magic wine was one of the few momentary sources of warmth that she could cherish.

"What else do you need, my queen?" chirped one of the Leekins, buzzing on tiny brown wings before her nose.

Lativia smiled. "I think it's time I checked on Sarah, don't you agree?"

The Leekin nodded excitedly and flew off into the woods. A huge bunch of Leekins soon returned, flying in formation to carry the weight of a glowing crystal ball. They lowered it to Lativia's lap, where it sank through the spectral outlines of her legs. Lativia could pass through things, and things could pass through her, for her physical body was long gone and all that remained was her powerful soul.

Lativia smiled even more broadly and began to draw her transparent ghostly hands over the ball, summoning the blood bond she shared with her descendent, Sarah Spellwood.

Gradually, the fog inside the ball began to clear and an image of Sarah's frizzy explosion of red curls filled it. Lativia drew back a few feet with her mind and saw Sarah was at a coffee shop ordering a vegan sandwich. Sarah's love and respect for animals always made Lativia proud. She noticed there was a conspicuous pale and indented band of skin on Sarah's ring finger where her huge diamond wedding ring had once been. "That no-good husband of hers is finally gone!" Lativia crowed with delight. But then she noticed that there were bags under Sarah's eyes, the bags of someone who had been up all night crying. *Sarah must be heartbroken*, Lativia thought with a heavy heart.

The barista serving Sarah froze when she saw Sarah's last name on the credit card receipt. "Um, are you related to . . . ?"

Sarah drearily raised her hand. "Yep, I'm descended from Lativia Spellwood."

"That's amazing! I mean, have you ever been to Witchland and looked at the Lativia memorabilia?" The barista's pigtails wiggled with her excited body language, and Lativia felt a swell of pride that people still remembered and even revered her. It had been four centuries and she was still honored as the greatest witch of New England, the one who had turned into a wolf and fought her way free of her captors at the Salem Witch Trials!

"Yep," Sarah said, her voice full of annoyance. It was clear she was ready to dash out of the coffee shop.

Lativa knew Sarah was a good lawyer but she noticed how awkward Sarah was around most people, and how little she liked to disclose personal details, especially of her magical ancestry. Sarah was a woman of facts and logic, which is why she fought the magical powers pulsing through her like a current, trying to pull her back to her destiny. Her resistance to her true self and her stubborn adherence to logical facts made her unpopular with many people. Lativia yearned to watch Sarah blossom into her beautiful potential.

"Don't you see?" Lativia cried. "You are not meant to be in New York! You should be here, following your calling, completing my work as a witch! You're not happy there!" But Sarah couldn't hear these words.

"Yes, yes," several Leekins agreed. A ghost who was standing near Lativia also nodded his head.

Sarah trudged out of the coffee shop, carrying her drink and the sandwich in a paper bag. A man in a trench coat bumped into her, and she hastily checked her pockets to ensure he had not pickpocketed anything. Then she continued on to her office, a massive steel gray prison with spikes in the window ledges to repel pigeons. There was no sign of life anywhere but for the scraggly maple planted out front of the building and a few waxy tropical plants blooming inside the lobby. Lativia groaned, feeling the despair and coldness of the place.

"It's time for you to come here, to your destined home," Lativia declared. "My Leekins have told me about the Hunter tracking lynx and the land surveyors, and I sense that there is about to be trouble in the forest."

At the mention of the Hunter, the Leekins gathered around her throne began to turn blue and tremble in terror.

"I am not strong enough to fight these battles much longer, so I need you to come home, to come into your true self. Your marriage fell apart of its own accord, and I sense your job is about to unravel on its own, too. You can't fight destiny," Lativia said, giving the group of hovering Leekins their crystal ball back and shutting her eyes. "I could use magic to bring you to your destiny sooner, but it is evil to interfere with one's life that way. I can only hope you don't take much longer."

She opened her eyes as the Leekins cried, "We need her!"

New York City top real estate attorney. Fierce redhead with green eyes. Direct descendent of Lativia Spellwood, a survivor of the Salem Witch Trials and the most notorious witch legend in New England. Sarah Spellwood was all of those things, and she thought she had life all figured out, until it fell apart before her very eyes.

The problems all started when the man Sarah had married ten years earlier approached her one evening after she got home from her law firm. Jeff looked at her with his steely gray eyes, not a hint of a smile on his smooth shaven face, and asked her for a divorce, plain and simple. His tone of voice sounded as if he was asking her where she wanted to go out for dinner. He then walked out the door without a hint of an explanation.

A few days later, his best friend, Lance, showed up. Sarah opened the door, curious to see him. "Is everything okay?" she asked.

"Yeah, I'm just here to get Jeff's clothes," Lance replied. He looked apologetic and wouldn't quite meet Sarah's eyes.

"Why is he doing this?" Sarah begged Lance.

Lance only looked at her with sympathy before sharply looking away. He shrugged. "He just said the spark is gone. I'm sorry, Sarah."

"Is there someone else?" she demanded.

"I don't think so. You know Jeff isn't that kind of guy. I really don't know anything else, or I would tell you." Lance shrugged apologetically again and went about boxing up Jeff's things.

There was no fight, no anger, no rebuilding the relationship, no marriage counseling. They had originally met in the quad of law school and had gone through late-night study sessions, finals crunches, bar exam anxiety, and friend drama together. Getting married had been an obvious choice, as they were best friends. Though work had often come between them over the past ten years, Sarah thought their marriage had been sound. They'd always been able to talk about their problems—analyzing and discussing before things got out of hand. But this was different. He simply walked out.

One of the main things Sarah loved about being a lawyer was the fact that she loved to talk and work things out. She had learned to separate her emotions from the facts early in her career and that had carried over into her married life whenever things got too heated between her and her husband. So why couldn't she get him to talk this time? And where had their love mysteriously gone? Surely there was another woman, but Sarah couldn't find out anything.

Sarah finally got a clue during the divorce proceedings. Jeff had filed on grounds of irreconcilable differences. He didn't speak to anyone unless he had to. Even her commanding green eyes couldn't get a rise out of her husband like they had in the past. But when the mediator asked him what he wanted of their shared assets, he snarked, "She can give me a lot more than this; Lord knows she makes more money than I do. She's always bragging about winning this case or that one." Then he glanced at her, his eyes blazing with hurt pride.

Sarah gaped at him. "Is that why you're doing this? Because I'm a better attorney than you?"

He refused to look at her or answer, telling her that she had guessed the reason. Recollections of his silence when she talked about winning a new case, the times he complained she didn't make him dinner because she had been late at the office, and even the times he grumbled that men teased him at his firm about how they ought to fire him and hire his wife instead, came tumbling back to her. How had she missed it after so long? She was normally so intuitive, yet with her own marriage, she had missed the signs.

So, Sarah gave him everything but the apartment, and he didn't contest that at all. It was clear she just wanted to be done with it all, to go start her new life. She heard he moved to Chicago shortly after the divorce and took a job at a new firm, where no one knew how talented his ex-wife was with real estate law.

As she trudged through the annoyance of changing her last name back from Lawrence to Spellwood, and enduring the excited looks from people who wanted to know if she was related to the infamous Lativia Spellwood, her hurt soon became replaced by a hot coal of rage that burned inside her heart, a sense of betrayal and a misguided rejection of love. As a Lawrence, she had been proud, and she had been able to avoid the looks and questions that had haunted her all of her life thanks to the Spellwood name. Now, she was single, thirty-five, and getting the looks and questions again. "So are you related to Lativia Spellwood? Really? Wow, so are you a witch, too?" She felt hurt and pathetic, and she couldn't face either emotion.

Unable to remain in her empty home all by herself, with no one to talk to about how her day had gone over

Thai takeout, she threw herself headlong into her work. She spent her nights at the law office and her days surrounded by cases and paperwork, taking comfort in the facts surrounding her. Because of her efficiency and workaholism, case after case was tossed her way, and she made sure she won every single one. Her clients and co-workers started to describe her as overly committed—in the scary, driven, borderline obsessed kind of way. By all standards, she was the most successful attorney at the firm. "Don't you know that all work and no play makes Jack a dull boy?" her boss would cajole her at times. Really, Sarah knew he just felt bad that she stayed later than he did every day.

Work hardly soothed her, however. She noticed people talking among themselves and falling silent when she entered a room. Feeling isolated and alone, she then threw herself into the gym. In the morning, she would run from her apartment to the sleek, modern fitness club she was a member. She would continue her running on the treadmills or hit an early morning spin class that would drench her completely in sweat. Her curly red hair would explode in frizz around her head like an untamed animal and she would fight to tame it in the locker room before running back home for break-fast. Then, after work, she would return to the weight room, or go for a jog around Central Park in the gath-ering dusk. On weekends, if she didn't have any work to catch up on, she would go back to the gym for another grueling workout with her boxing coach.

In time, the hot coal faded to an ember. Sarah had relentless drive, but it now came more from momentum than rage. Sure, she smarted when she thought of Jeff, but she no longer searched for him in the faces of passersby or imagined him in place of her punching bag at the gym. And she finally stopped looking longingly at her phone at night, hoping it might light up with his name on the caller ID. As a prestigious lawyer potentially making partner any day now, boasting six-pack abs and a mean lightning left hook, Sarah felt more invincible than anything. Work was going spectacularly, as she took on more and more extra tasks, and she felt life was finally going well. Even so, something felt off, but she had enough distractions to ignore that gnawing feeling in her gut.

It felt like any other morning when Sarah jogged home from the gym one early summer day, almost a year since the divorce. Getting ready for work, Sarah prepared her favorite vegan breakfast: freshly cooked quinoa, roasted sweet potatoes, onions, and a pinch of cinnamon. To that, she added something that had her mouth watering on the way home from her workout—a bowl of fresh organic fruit from her neighborhood fruit stand.

When she reached her office, her phone rang as

soon as the elevator doors slid shut behind her. "Sarah, I would like to talk to you. Please come to my office immediately," her boss said briskly and hung up without any explanation.

He doesn't usually call me personally. His assistant must not be in yet. Could this be in reference to finally making me partner? Her stomach filled with butterflies, and she imagined Spellwood added to the line of names in gold letters on the lobby wall.

Sarah strode into her boss's office, straightening her blazer and wondering how to react to the news. That was surely what this impromptu meeting was regarding.

Mr. Emmett smiled at her coolly. "Sarah, take a seat." He gestured to the gray chair positioned across from him. As Sarah sat, he launched immediately into his speech: "I am sorry to say this, Sarah, but we have to furlough you for a few weeks."

Sarah gaped at him. "What?" she finally managed to stammer out gracelessly.

"It's just not fair to the other lawyers," Mr. Emmett added, attempting to look sympathetic as greed shone behind his eyes. "You're a talented lawyer, but we can't have you taking all the clients just because you have more time since your divorce."

"What? This is ridiculous. It doesn't make any sense. I'm your best lawyer and get the most work done around here," protested Sarah, still struggling to regain her poise. Her green eyes pierced those of her boss, which caused him to look down at the floor.

"It is what it is, Sarah, and that's all there is to it. There is nothing else to talk about."

"I think there is." Sarah seethed. "I think this is because I'm a woman."

He scoffed. "If I were a sexist, would I have hired you?"

"You hired me to fill out your diversity requirement. You didn't actually expect me to excel. I've been here years and I've never felt appreciated. I'm always passed over for your male lawyers," Sarah went on.

He sighed. "The only reason I passed you over was because you—how shall I put this—you don't strike me as a leader. You're not management material. You have always had a bit of trouble connecting to people."

"Really? If that were so, then how do I win every case I take and settle most of them before we have to go to court?" Sarah felt herself start shaking.

"Sarah, there is really nothing more to talk about. I've made my decision. Now you can go back to your office and start preparing your open cases for me to take over. I have things to do," he said, still not making eye contact.

She slowly stood and returned to her office, feeling gut wrenched. This job was her everything! *Another man that can't tell me what the hell is going on. I am so done with all of this.*

As Sarah began to go through her files, it hit her. "This is all just a thinly veiled attempt by my boss to hone in on my clients and take the pay all for himself. And talk about the male chauvinism! Just like Jeff, he can't stand a woman who succeeds."

In an angry rage, she stormed back into his office. He was on the phone and stared at her with annoyance as she flung his door open, ignoring the feeble protests of his secretary. "You know what? You take my cases and my clients for good. After all I have done for you and this firm, and all of the money I have made for you with my blood, sweat, and tears, I have never been so insulted in my life! I quit!"

Pausing only to collect her things, she said goodbye to a few friends and then walked out of her old work life for good.

CHAPTER TWO

Sarah was now a recently divorced lawyer out of a job. The realization hit her as she hurried home. *Geez, I have that feeling again . . . that my bad day is not over yet,* she thought, bumping into her mailman as he opened the door to her building.

"Here ya go, Sarah. Here's all your mail for today," he said, handing her mostly junk mail. "I'll give it to you now instead of putting it in your mailbox."

"Oh come on, Stanley. I know there's more. Stop playing that game with me."

"Seriously, Sarah, this time there is no more mail for you. Your guess is wrong this time." Stanley laughed while hoisting his mail bag to his right shoulder.

Hmm, something is not right. As soon as I bumped into Stanley, I had this weird tingling. If it's not more mail, then what could it be? I am definitely not attracted to my mailman, so my tingling sensation isn't for him! she thought as she pushed the button in the elevator for her floor.

Getting out of the elevator and walking down the hall, Sarah looked up to find her former mentor's dog tied to her apartment door. There was an envelope taped above the handle.

What the heck? she thought, tucking the envelope in her back pocket, thinking Michael was inside.

"Hey, Addie." She smiled at the panting dog that jumped up enthusiastically to greet her. Addie's wet nose pointed at her pocket with the envelope as Sarah petted her. Sarah had always had a thing for animals, and she especially loved the dog in front of her now. Her fur was silky soft with the most beautiful shade of gold. And her personality was perfection—smart and intuitive coupled with just the right amount of independence. The perfect golden-collie mix.

It was as if fate had sent her Addie to help her forget all the troubles she'd just waded through.

"Addie? Why are you outside my door and not in the apartment? What is it, girl? Did Michael leave you with me for the weekend, honey? Did he leave you without telling me first?" Sarah didn't mind if Michael had. After all, it wasn't like she had a job to worry about anymore. And Michael Howler was her dearest friend, someone she would do anything for.

She quickly peeked into her apartment. "Michael, are you in here? Michael?" No answer. *He must be talking to one of the neighbors, and for some bizarre reason, didn't take her with him,* Sarah thought while noticing that tingling feeling again.

With Addie prancing perfectly by her side, she walked down the hall and knocked on the doors of each of the apartments in her building. Nothing. Nobody had seen anyone fitting his description.

She ran down the hall, looked down the staircase, and checked the elevator, hoping he would pop out at any minute. "I wonder where he is. He takes you every-where, Addie."

She went back downstairs to the front-door stoop, sat down, and thought about her former teacher. Michael had been her legal mentor for almost fifteen years; he taught her everything she needed to know about real estate, attorneys, and the practice of law. He was a kind man who not only believed in the law but also in the goodness of people. He never took law cases out of any sort of malice or greed, unlike her now ex-boss. He simply had a strong desire to help people get their affairs in order and understand their basic rights and responsibilities.

He was not your typical lawyer but more of a

teacher, helping his clients understand their cases by cutting the legalese and courtroom jargon down to a bare minimum. 'Goodbye confusion, hello clarity' was Michael's byline. This usually translated into a straight-shooting and useful plan where his clients could work with him and help to defend themselves. It was a win-win situation.

The fact was Michael had changed his life about ten years ago, leaving the city devoid of one of its finest lawyers, and leaving Sarah with a wealth of knowledge but not too many people skills. After Sarah showed him pictures of Witchland, the town her ancestor Lativia Spellwood had founded, Michael took off there for a trip. A week later, he came back, declaring that he had found a house and was moving there.

"Why? You won't have many clients," Sarah protested, thinking back on how small the town had been when she had visited her aunt there for summers as a little girl.

"It's time for me to get in touch with myself and deepen my magical practice," he had replied. "Don't worry, I'll still visit, and you can visit me. Get out of the city for a while, breathe some fresh air. Besides, if you ever need a new perspective on a case, I'm just a call away."

Michael would sometimes send her letters from there or call and give her advice on tough cases, and sometimes he would appear at her apartment with his dog, Addie, when she needed to be watched. Michael would stay for a bit, but he'd always leave soon, to tackle some "magical mystery" or go help someone on a case for free.

Since Sarah had met him, Michael had been interested in all things paranormal, something Sarah had once loved as a kid but now dismissed with a roll of her eyes. But he seemed happy, and that was what mattered. She often thought of him as a wandering hero in one of the novels she loved to read, always going around helping people, especially with their more paranormal issues. He had wanted to assist as many people as possible, and although he was aiding scores of clients as a real estate lawyer, he always had a desire to be of assistance to them personally as well. Getting rid of ghosts, helping people talk to lost loved ones, offering them sage advice on magical troubles—whatever people needed, he did for them.

Hopefully, he was back now, because she desperately needed his advice and his counsel. Maybe he could help her view her life as a complicated legal case, with a simple solution. That was always the best way to tackle life problems, Sarah had learned over the years.

"All right, Addie, let's go back inside and double-check the apartment. Maybe he was in the bathroom and didn't hear us." Sarah sighed before moving to open her door again.

Walking back inside to her apartment, she remarked to Addie, "The world needs more lawyers like Michael, and if it had more of them, maybe I wouldn't be here right now. Maybe I'd still be making money as an attorney and helping people learn about their rights and how to fight for them."

Sarah continued, "Yet, Michael would never leave you at the entrance to my apartment with an envelope taped to my door. Something is just not right."

Addie barked and shot inside as Sarah opened her door. Sarah groaned when she didn't see Michael after a more thorough check of the apartment. Usually, he would be sitting on her sofa, helping himself to her food and listening to her vast collection of music.

It looked like he had just dropped Addie off and gone back on the road. "This is not the typical Michael I know," Sarah said to Addie. She shook her head and opened the letter, fully expecting to see her responsibilities to Addie as well as an update on Michael's life in his scrawled handwriting, only to pull out a letter that was anything but that.

For one thing, the paper was different. When Michael had written to her previously, he'd done it on postcards or scraps of whatever paper he had on hand. This note was on business paper, the same paper he always used as a lawyer, and there was something else inside.

"A will," she whispered hesitantly as she unfolded the second sheet of paper, praying this was all some sick joke as she read through it. Yet her training in law had taught her to recognize the formatting of a real will and what to pick out as she read through it.

Michael was dead, and Sarah was the named beneficiary to inherit the law practice he had founded in Witchland.

A single silver key fell into her trembling palm as she sunk to the floor, staring at Addie as she swallowed hard. *Some people just seemed like they would never die, and Michael was one of them. He has always been there when I was learning law, or when I was staying up at night working on a case, or trying to solve a real estate mystery. He was usually there with a pot of coffee and some wise words that made the answer seem clear.* "This is horrible, Addie." Sarah felt as if she had been punched in the gut; as tears rose in her eyes, she struggled to breathe.

As Sarah began to tear up, Addie licked her hand and gazed up with her brown eyes, those canine orbs seeming wiser than ever. Sarah unfolded the last note in the envelope to be confronted with her old mentor's handwriting.

Hello Sarah,

If you are reading this, it means I am dead, and all my files and clients have been passed to you. Much like in my life, I have prepared for everything in my death. The key opens my office in Witchland, New Hampshire. I don't know if you want to move to this town and continue my work, but I hope you do. I know I can't control that fiery mind of yours, but if you don't take control of my legacy, it will be ruined by my rival, a Mr. John Gonforth, who is as much of a shady lawyer as he is a terrible man.

Regardless of what you choose, Addie, my files and clients and various other holdings of mine are now yours. You were always my favorite student, so I know everything is in good hands.

And if you take me up on this offer, I can promise you, you will come to feel like Witchland is your home. You will return to your childhood in many ways and be happier than you ever have been in New York. I can't tell you the details now, but if everything goes as I hope, you will eventually know you made the right choice.

Keep making the world better,
Michael

Sarah took a deep breath and ran her fingers through Addie's fur, blinking back tears. "Michael taught me everything I know. He made me the lawyer I am today, and now he is gone. And on top of that, he has asked me to give up everything and move to a town I haven't been to in almost twenty years, since Aunt Beth died," whispered Sarah.

"Typical Michael, right, Addie?" She sighed before standing up and putting the items from the envelope on her counter. "Always asking for the unexpected at the perfect time. But something about this is off, Addie. How did he die? And so suddenly?" The name John Gonforth stood out in her mind.

As Addie sniffed around the large apartment, Sarah took a deep breath. Her mind started to weigh out the options presented in front of her, arranging them like a case.

She was divorced, out of a job, and had just lost her dearest friend suddenly. What else did New York have to offer her except the bitter cocktail of bad memories it currently forced down her throat?

Suddenly, Addie stopped near the front door. Whining with her nose to the ground and tail wagging in an anxious circle, she looked back up at Sarah with her brown eyes demanding attention. She barked at Sarah once and put her nose deliberately back down to the ground. "What are you doing, Addie?" Again, Addie barked, but this time she went up to Sarah, inviting her to follow her. "Okay, what is it, girl?"

Sarah looked down to where Addie's determined nose pointed and there to the right of the closed door of her apartment was a flat scrap of paper that she had missed before. Leaning over to pick it up, she looked over at Addie. Sarah could have sworn she saw a smile on Addie's face.

"Addie, I wonder who left this note? Because this sure as hell is not Michael's handwriting." Holding the paper in front of Addie's face and hers, she read: "Michael was murdered. Please help us."

After a good long while of consideration and thought, Sarah finally said, "Addie, if someone murdered Michael, then I am going to find out who."

Grabbing a suitcase and looking around the sizable apartment she had once shared with her husband, she began to pack just what would fit inside it.

CHAPTER THREE

THE FIVE-HOUR DRIVE TO WITCHLAND IN HER NEW Beamer wasn't too bad. Sarah had lots of music to listen to, a great dog for company, and plenty of time to think about what she was leaving behind—a demanding, high-stakes job; a greedy, unreasonable boss; and a sleazy ex-husband who didn't respect her enough to tell her the truth. Everything she wanted to keep was stuffed in the back of her car as she headed for a completely new future, with only a key to Michael's office and a scribbled note in messy handwriting stating he was murdered to keep her focused.

"I'm ready to start over, but this note is really weird. I am going to figure out who wrote it and why Michael was murdered," she said as she stroked Addie's fur. "I promise, girl."

Before she left, she had done her research about

Witchland, since she couldn't trust her childhood memories as an accurate picture of the town. She had the basic facts about the small town down. It seemed quiet enough, with about two thousand people living in and around it, so nothing at all like the city. There was a coffee shop, a gym, and some local businesses that kept the townsfolk going.

She sighed at the town's name as her car passed the 'Welcome to Witchland' sign. "Witchland," she ruminated. "If I see anyone either dressed up like a witch with a pointy hat or anyone shorter than four feet, we are turning around without another word. Are you with me, Addie?" Vague memories of such sights from her previous summer visits returned to her, as well as memories of the strange garments and items like cauldrons stashed in her aunt's attic, which she and her parents had cleaned out after her passing.

Sarah smiled down at her companion, who was in the front seat. Addie wagged her tail happily as she turned from the open window. "I might need to change my name, or I'll get mobbed if anyone guesses I am a descendant of Lativia Spellwood." Since Lativia Spellwood had founded Witchland in the 1600s, it had become a haven for her modern-day groupies.

The rest of her drive was completed in deep contemplation, wondering what had happened to Michael, until she suddenly found herself right smack in the middle of the town square. She parked her car in a designated parking area, and soon both she and Addie were stretching their legs as they looked around at the small town. "Wow, Addie. This is as beautiful as I remembered. Let's walk around a little."

"Excuse me, but could you give me directions to Michael Howler's law office?" she asked while peering down at a fellow passerby. Mustering up every inch of her self-control, she thought, *Oh my God, there are elves and witches in this town. This woman is wearing a slouchy hat that literally has a pointed end that touches the middle of her back. This is probably just the latest fashion statement in this town.*

"Sure, just keep going. It's on your left next to the large greenhouse. Wow, you are a tall one, aren't you? And it isn't those five-inch city-slicker shoes you are wearing. They call those Jimmy *Choose* shoes, don't they?"

Despite her first interaction, her judgy thought, and the snarky comment about her Jimmy Choos, Sarah smiled as she walked through the streets, taking in the town's beauty. But she felt her anxiety build a little because the first person she saw was indeed a little on the short side, and sported a questionable hat style—could she be a witch after all?

Sarah was in awe of what her eyes were taking in. Witchland was entirely surrounded by National Forest and was perfectly situated near a clear, cold-running brook. Apparently, the locals took pride in this and maintained a very attractive town square. "This is wonderful—just what I need for my new life." Smiling, she strolled along with Addie down the sidewalks of this beautiful town.

Signs and shops boasted about all their furniture being made by hand at the local sawmill that recycled all of its wood products or about the vast gardens that provided a plethora of vegetables at the daily farmer's market.

It was as if this town respected the land as a living and breathing entity and was soundly rewarded for its efforts. Unlike the city, where people covered up nature with concrete and steel with no concern for its creatures, here it was allowed to grow and flourish alongside the people and the buildings. Vines crept over stone and brick, flowers peeked from every nook and cranny, and trees lined the main street that went through the town and crowded around each business and house. Sarah remembered certain businesses and the strange, witchy script on signs, like the Javacadabra coffee shop where her parents and Aunt Beth liked to go. "I could really get used to this place again," Sarah said happily, humming as she walked down the street next to a park. She noticed the woman in the pointy hat waving to her and smiling.

"Oh, Addie, this is beautiful. I can understand why this was such a retreat for Michael. I can't imagine anything bad happening in this town, especially someone murdering Michael," Sarah said aloud.

Addie barked, almost in response, and wagged her tail. Sarah had a brief memory of a talking goat on her aunt's little farm, and quickly pushed the memory away. Animals didn't talk like humans!

Looking around, she noticed how the town hall graced the center of the town and was surrounded by various homes, shops, and other residential buildings. A police station rested just behind Town Hall, and a doctor's office sat just across from that. All of the buildings had older New England stone architecture, with neatly painted trim; they could have been from the early 1800s just as well as now. "It's nice to see everything is within walking distance," Sarah mused as she noticed the location of a small grocery as well. Addie pointed her snout toward the grocery and licked her chops, clearly relishing the scent of the lamb chops and ribeyes on special.

The homes she passed all had magnificent wooden lawn furniture resting on their porches, and some of the chairs and tables creaked as their occupants lazily gazed upon Sarah and Addie as they walked by. More than a few of them called out, "Hello," or lifted their hands in serene greeting, even though they had no clue who Sarah was. One woman called out, "Hi, Addie!" and Addie greeted her with a vigorous tail wag. Sarah was used to the city life, where people were in too much of a hurry to bother to get to know each other, or to even bother to care. Most people in New York walked around with permanent scowls on their faces, their brusque and abrasive attitudes practically tangible. But here, people seemed to have nowhere to rush to, and their warmth overflowed. Sarah realized she would have to get used to that if she were going to make this place her home.

Sarah was awed by the number of chimes and birdhouses that seemed to hang from every tree inside the town. "You wouldn't find this in the city, Addie," Sarah said with a smile as the sounds of the wind chimes and chirping birds filled her ears. It was such a pleasant sound, compared to honking gridlocked traffic and the squealing of subway trains.

It was as if something more powerful—like nature herself—was guiding Sarah through the town—a familiar feeling that she had rejected for so long. It felt incredible. She had not even realized how much she had missed the smells, the sights, the sounds, the sensation of life itself, that reverberated through the town. It wasn't just nice to look at; it was nice for her soul. She drank it in, feeling herself begin to heal already. *Thank you, Michael.*

She loved the sparsely populated streets and the friendliness of the passersby. All kinds of interesting people were either engaged in conversation or delighted to stop to introduce themselves to her and to pet Addie. And to Sarah's relief, none of them were under four feet, dressed in witch's garb, or made reference to her last name.

All is good so far, she thought, keeping her eyes on the scenery and the friendly faces.

In the span of five minutes, she had responded to more hellos and shaken more hands than she would have in five hours in New York. Her heart warmed when people stopped her to talk about Michael, offer their condolences, and welcome her to town. Especially when they revealed that they knew about her being his best apprentice, too, regaling her with stories that her mentor had told about her. It seemed as if everyone already knew exactly who she was; they had clearly been expecting her. Michael must have been bragging about her, which made her chest puff out in pride.

Some of the stories people brought up about her and Michael were so old she'd even forgotten about them, but as the locals told her about her own exploits, her heart swelled with a fondness for the brilliant man. Her brain instantly recorded the new versions of the stories she had forgotten, locking them away to be examined at another time.

It was apparent that Michael was well loved and an integral part of this community. "Well, Addie, looks like you and Michael made some friends here," she remarked after a group of small children had swarmed Addie with cuddles and pets, obviously recognizing her.

After spending some time chatting with a former client of Michael's, Sarah moved on toward Michael's office and got caught up in her thoughts about New York, Witchland, and all the recent events in her life. She inhaled the sweet-smelling miasma of blooming flowers all around her and felt giddy. Was this really happening? Life for the past ten years flashed before her eyes, and made her wonder how all of this had happened. She was grieving Michael and also celebrating a new start. What a whirlwind of emotions! She was so busy thinking that she failed to notice she was on a collision course with another passerby, when —BAM!—she slammed right into his chest. The blow was harder than expected, causing her to let out an undignified shriek as she bounced backward.

Sarah had almost reached the ground when a pair of strong arms wrapped around her waist and caught her, then held her steady as she got back on her feet.

As she lifted her eyes to gaze at her rescuer, she found herself utterly breathless.

There in front of her was a tall, slender man whose muscles could be seen behind the thin outline of his uniform. He had icy blue eyes that stood out among his black and gorgeous curly hair. His perfectly white smile shined like a miniature sun as he released her from his grip. His hands lingered on her waist, though, ensuring she was completely steady before he stepped backward and exclaimed, "Are you okay?" in a voice way too deep to be legal.

"Y—yeah," she answered, twisting her left earring while collecting her feet back under herself as she took a deep breath. *What the hell am I doing twisting my earring again—for a man?* she scolded herself as she quickly lowered her hand. This annoying habit had developed with her first high school crush, a gorgeous lacrosse player who had rejected her for a cheerleader. But that was eighteen years ago! Yet, she couldn't shake her gut feeling—she was attracted to this man that stood before her. The flowery miasma of the town was enough to put her to sleep, and this man's smile was enough to instantly wake her up like a shot of espresso from her favorite bistro in New York. Struggling hard not to blush or stutter, she sucked in a breath and smiled. "I—I—I'm okay."

Her eyes instantly noticed the policeman's star

pinned to his blue uniform on his muscular chest. "Just trying to find my way to the office of Michael Howler. I am—er—*was* his apprentice and I am now in line to take over his office," she added, trying not to sound like a professional woman who had lost her composure.

"Of course. Sarah Spellwood." He grinned graciously. "You'll find it just down there. Surely it was a shame what happened to him," the policeman added, gently placing a hand on her shoulder to maneuver her in the right direction, causing an entire forest of butterflies to rise up in her stomach. "I'm the police chief of this little slice of paradise. Name's Eli Strongheart. I can't tell you how many times Michael and I went for coffee and talked over the cases we were working on."

She smiled, trying not to notice how nice his hand felt on her shoulder. No man had touched her . . . well, since before Jeff had left. They had not been very physically affectionate, and she often found herself longing for Jeff to at least touch her hand when they sat on the couch reading papers and books together in the evening. "Do you know how Michael died?"

"Yes, he appeared to have fallen down the stairs," Eli replied.

Sarah was startled to see how the policeman seemed to think it was an accident. She thought of the disturbing note on the floor and had to turn away for a second to hide her tears. She watched Addie dart ahead to sniff at the ground, bored with the humans' conversation as she investigated the new scents on the street. "Oh, no," sniffled Sarah, tears already spilling over slightly. "He taught me everything I know about real estate law, and he was such a good friend. I will be lost without him. The way he died just doesn't make sense to me. Michael was in really good shape, and I have this note that was slipped under my front door."

"Yes, Michael is going to be missed here in Witchland. He was an all-around good guy and great attorney," Eli agreed. He accepted the note and glanced at it, before furrowing his brow in concern. "The coroner's report didn't show anything other than a fall, so we ruled his death as an accident. But this note is troubling. Hopefully it's a prank, but I will keep it as evidence just in case."

"Please do. I really don't believe he just died from a fall. Michael wasn't old, and as I said, he was in great shape. With all due respect, I hope you would look into this more and give Michael the justice he deserves, Officer Eli. Well, in any case, I guess there'll be a new real estate attorney in his office now," lamented Sarah, not sure if she was going to cry or pass out from the news or start yelling at this handsome hunk to take her seriously about the murder note.

"Then you'll have to meet John Gonforth. He's another real estate attorney in town. He and Michael were fierce competitors for any scrap of business they could get since we really don't get too many people who need their services. John was pretty ugly when it came to Michael, but Michael was always a gentleman and never got caught up in petty competition." Eli added, "When you're ready to meet him, you can find his office next to the sawmill."

Sarah thanked him and then watched him walk away, admiring how perfectly his black pants fit him. He was such a hunk. Too bad he didn't think Michael had been murdered! "Geesh, he changed the subject super quick on me." Sarah sighed extra loud while she looked down at Addie. "And calling the note a prank? Who would play such a prank on me? Someone wouldn't bring you all of the way to New York and leave that note as a prank. It had to be someone close to Michael, someone who knew him here."

Sarah turned the corner and saw Michael's office. It was a little house, but the sign declaring 'Michael Howler, Attorney at Law' was impossible to miss. The house and its front garden were stunning, and she could definitely see herself living there. The outside gardens were vibrant and colorful with butterflies, bees, and dragonflies making themselves at home among sprays of colorful flowers.

"Addie, your home is breathtaking," Sarah exclaimed. "I can see why Michael's clients loved visiting him." Taking in as much as she could while gazing at her potential new home and office, Sarah recalled that, in law school, one of Michael's first lessons as her professor was about building trust with clients. She fondly remembered him saying, "Adjust to get trust or your business will go bust."

Sarah tried numerous times to create an office space she loved at the firm in New York, but her boss would have nothing to do with it. Everything had to look the same, even down to the color of the paper clips. Michael's office was just the opposite, rich with character and natural beauty, and she couldn't wait to get inside.

While walking up the fieldstone walkway to Michael's office door, she saw the smaller sign on his door:

Michael Howler
Real Estate Attorney
Need a Clear Title You Can Lien On?

She chuckled to herself. She loved the way her mentor tended to turn legal words and truisms into actions. He was always teaching her to stand out among the other attorneys by using her humor and other quirks that most attorneys lacked. His class was the only fun one out of all of her law classes in three years of law school.

As Sarah walked up the steps, her thoughts turned back to that police chief she just met. Resisting the urge to twist her left earring, she said out loud, "My, what a handsome man." While she was not one to wish for crime, she might just have to come up with a good reason to see more of him.

"Come on, Addie." Sarah smiled, patting her legs as she stepped onto the porch and turned her key in the lock, opening the wooden door with a creak.

THE AGED WOODEN DOOR TO MICHAEL'S HOME didn't say much about the appearance of the inside, but once the door was opened and the sun shined through, Sarah could see the interior was stunningly well appointed.

Addie followed Sarah inside as she walked through the cozy living room which also served as a client meeting room. She opened the door on the far side of the room that led to a large room in the back which she knew was the office; she chuckled slightly as she saw the complete disarray that was prominent in every office Michael had ever owned.

"Addie, this is the part of Michael I never understood. The outside of his home and receiving area is gorgeous, but his workspace is a disaster." She shook her head disapprovingly, her sense of tidiness making her want to reorganize the room immediately. How he was able to work in such chaos was beyond her. Files were organized haphazardly in cabinets and stacked on desks, chairs, and anything else that constituted a flat surface, all in an apparently ordered pattern that he never shared with anyone. Papers and diagrams were pinned to a large cork board in the center of the far wall and were connected to one another with different colors of string; when Sarah surveyed it, it made no sense whatsoever. The whole place desperately needed a meeting with a duster and a vacuum, not to mention a filing expert.

Simply walking into the room caused her to sneeze violently, upending the dust bunnies that had taken refuge in every corner of the room. She waved her hand in front of her face to scatter a few lingering cobwebs as she crossed the room with one final shuffle. "How long had it been since Michael sent that letter, and how did Addie and the letter get to me?" grumbled Sarah as she pulled the cobwebs out of her eyes.

"Addie, all of this is really strange to me and I can't put my finger on it. This house is a mess, and I am feeling some very weird vibes here suddenly. I know Michael isn't the most organized and when we worked together during my apprentice days, the man barely stopped to eat or rest. Ya know Addie, I think it's

Michael letting me know that something bad happened to him here."

Sarah reminisced, *Along with being his assistant, I almost became his glorified maid.*

If she wasn't learning legal terms or having Michael coach her on how to finish a case, she was constantly heating up meals for the both of them or ensuring their workspaces were relatively clean. Normally, she would have objected to this regimen, but with Michael, she knew it was worth being around his brilliant mind and putting up with the occasional grunt work.

After she outgrew her apprenticeship at the office, he regressed into the workaholic lifestyle that left little time for cleanliness or orderliness. As she surveyed the scene, she was thankful that while she had adopted his workaholic tendencies, she had not taken on his tendency toward chaos as well.

Addie barked and laid down in the center of the room. Her tail thumped on the ground and sent more dust up as she made herself comfortable despite the mess. Sarah poked around the room for a while and then headed up a set of stairs that led to a bedroom and bathroom. The bathroom was sizable and acted as a weird little backup kitchen. It even had a small refrigerator filled with various frozen meals and a microwave to cook them in. Some were even the healthy ones she had bought him and packed in his empty cooler the last time he was in New York.

Michael always did like to be close to food, she mused to herself, noticing the microwave was remarkably clean, unlike everything else.

After inspecting the rest of the makeshift kitchen, Sarah walked back downstairs to the living room and sat down in the old rocking chair next to a window with a wonderful view of the forest. It was one of the few places not covered in dust or files.

"At least Michael kept his client meeting room in tip-top shape." Sarah sighed as she opened the window and melted into the warm and inviting atmosphere. "But I keep having this feeling that something is not right in this house."

She could hear the breeze gently swaying the trees and grass, punctuated by the chirping birds and buzzing bees. Mesmerized, Sarah gave in to the wave of exhaustion that coursed through her body. For what seemed like an eternity, but was actually only a few seconds, she drank in the tranquil landscape and meditated on what it must have been like for Michael as he sat there and looked out upon the world. All this was making her feel a bit out of place. Even though Witchland was stunningly beautiful, she was a city girl who was denied access to the natural world by her parents early on in life. They wanted her to be successful, so every moment of her time was funneled into books, lessons, and homework once she hit middle school. She didn't even notice if it was sunny or rainy most days when she was too buried in books throughout her later childhood. Sighing, she told the dog, "Addie, it is time for me to take off these heels and enjoy what is here."

Addie walked over and nuzzled her hand, seeming to enjoy the moment as much as Sarah was. Sarah smiled. Her hand moved over Addie's head, and she immediately felt calm as Addie looked at her with soulful eyes.

"I can see why you and Michael liked it here." She sighed, leaning back and letting the old chair creak gently back on its rockers. "Heck, this place is even starting to get to me with all these serene landscapes and friendly people walking around. Not to mention that handsome police officer. I just wish I had more answers. How did Michael die, girl? Was he really murdered, or was that a sick joke like Eli thinks? How did you get to my home? What am I supposed to do now?" As the thoughts churned in her mind, she felt her eyelids grow heavy. A bumblebee buzzed right outside the open window. Sarah smiled, feeling herself fading out of consciousness.

The doorbell interrupted her sleep. She stood up, shaking herself a bit as she walked toward the door, refreshed her bright red lipstick she kept in her pocket, and opened it, wondering if Eli—that astoundingly handsome police officer—had come to visit her. That would be a welcome visit indeed.

Instead, she was greeted by a seedy-looking man in a rumpled brown business suit, complete with a big bald spot in his receding brown hair and a thin mustache, as he smiled at her from behind thick black glasses. "Hello, Sarah. I'm John Gonforth, a real estate attorney in Witchland. Word travels fast in this town, so I figured I'd come by and introduce myself. May I come in?"

"I don't thi—" Sarah tried to say as Addie cowered away and lowered her tail.

"Great!" John smiled, shoving the door open and walking inside despite Addie's growls. "Oh, settle down, pooch. This won't take long.

"Sarah, I came to tell you that we are going to make history in this town, you and I. Right now, I'm working on a deal with some brilliant developers to transform the forest into a gorgeous suite of condos, stores, and malls. A massive hotel to finally offer visitors a place to stay is the first project on my list, for Pete's sake. In short order, we'll be the premiere destination town in New Hampshire. People will come from miles around for an exclusive vacation in the heart of Witchland. There'll be real estate deals galore for both you and me, just you wait and see.

"Sadly, Michael, may he rest in peace—I can't believe he fell down the stairs in his home," he added, looking down for a brief moment out of respect. "Well, anyway, Michael fought hard to oppose the wheels of progress. He wanted that decrepit old forest protected for some reason, and apparently, he didn't believe that trees could grow elsewhere in town, or that wood could be imported, or that things didn't need to be handmade or recycled. Golly, by building a beautiful development right next to the village, we will create a premiere resort town. Now *that's* where the money is."

John raised his hands to cut off Sarah's words of protest before giving her a thin-lipped smile. "So, Sarah, will you join me in allowing progress to come to this town and money to start flowing, or are you Michael's sidekick through and through, right down to his misguided ideals?"

Sarah walked toward the ringing phone, trying to keep her temper intact as she turned to face John, real-izing that his respect for Michael was just a facade. He'd burst into her home and barely let her get a word in edgewise, just like her old boss in New York.

Only this time she could do something about it. "Mr. Gonforth, respectfully, I don't appreciate your attitude toward my late friend, or you barging in with some get-rich-quick scheme. It'd be a cold day in hell before I'd do business with someone who has such little respect for Michael, the forest, or the beauty of this town. Now if you excuse me, I need to take this call."

John raised his hands in appeasement as Addie continued her low growl while walking forward with hackles raised. "No need to be huffy, Sarah. I'm just giving you a chance to make the right decision. You'll need to pick a side sooner or later, and I just wanted you to pick the one that's best for both of us, that's all."

Seeing Addie's menacing approach, the man quickly backed out the door, closing it behind him as Addie began wagging her tail in triumph.

"Hey, girl, didn't we tell him a thing or two? Thanks for helping scare him away. That call was the wrong number but it came at a perfect time." Sarah congratulated Addie by petting her scruff and scratching her chest. "Here I was, hoping that this would be a boring little town where nothing would ever happen. Fat chance. I could have used a small vacation, though, and something a little more peaceful in my life."

As she thought about what John had said, she began to feel that weird *witchy* feeling again—and this time the hair on her neck prickled. Turning back to look through Michael's things, she couldn't help but wonder what exactly her mentor had gotten himself— and her—into. What was Gonforth really after? Did he really want to join with her in handling all the real estate deals, or was this just a ruse to get what he wanted without her opposition? How is it that Michael had just died and Gonforth was already pushing his agenda with the development? Were the two related at all?

CHAPTER FIVE

Before Sarah could do anything else, she had to calm down. John's visit had thoroughly rattled her nerves and set off her intuition that something was wrong. There was no way in hell she was going to let this jerk get the best of her. "How dare he talk about Michael that way?" she hissed out loud as she mentally reviewed the details of her first meeting with John Gonforth.

Gonforth was seedy-looking, aggressive, and had pushed right into the house as if he owned it. There was nothing cordial or respectful about him. "He couldn't care less about me or what I thought. All he wanted to do was sway my opinion in favor of his development. Thank heavens he knew enough to back out when he did. He seems like the kind of guy capable of murder, right?"

"You did a great job, Addie," Sarah continued. "You know, Addie, if I were in New York, I'd know exactly what to do with a tough opponent, but I'm not totally sure what I can do here in Witchland. I don't even have anyone I can trust to back me up here."

Her green eyes furiously flicked around the room as she hoped against hope that Michael would somehow materialize and give her some sound advice. But she knew that wasn't going to happen. More and more, she was realizing what a giant hole his passing had left in her life, and her heart ached.

"You are a great listener, Addie," she said. "But, thankfully, you don't have to deal with people like John Gonforth. You are *so* lucky you're a dog because people can be so weird sometimes."

Addie shot Sarah a sideward glance as she nestled into the dog bed in the corner of the room by the old rocking chair. Taking a cue from Addie, Sarah plopped down in the rocking chair by the window once again. She then spent about ten minutes calming her nerves while rocking herself back and forth as she gazed out the window. The forest seemed to look back at her, calm and serene, as a birdsong wafted across the warm summer air.

I wonder if that deceitful lawyer ever bothered to look at this view? she thought, questioning why anyone would think about destroying this beautiful forest to build a bunch of hotels, big-box stores, and ugly strip malls. Her memories here, of quiet, languid summers and itchy mosquito bites and fireflies in jars, were unchallenged by the present; nothing much had changed, and Sarah appreciated that. Everything in life changed far too much, and everything was covered in concrete in far too much of the country. Having this little town, with its natural landscape and old architecture, was a blessing. She sensed she was not the only one who felt that way here. The quaint and natural resourcefulness of its people was the lifeblood of Witchland, and John was attempting to change it, even *kill* it, by turning it into something else. It was clear that he had plans to rob Witchland of its beauty and uniqueness—all for money, profit, and apparent control of the businesses in town.

The doorbell rang again, pulling her out of her deep thoughts. As she stood up and walked to answer it, Addie was right at her heels, barking and sniffing the air excitedly.

Opening the door, Sarah saw vegetables—a lot of them. Then she noticed the two smiling women dressed in overalls with big woolly socks stuffed into their flat sandals, proffering a huge basket of produce. The shorter of the two had her hair in a neat black bob with strands of gray in it; the taller one wore a blonde braid down to her waist. Their gardening gloves were stained with dirt in the creases.

"Hello," they both echoed kindly.

"We're your new neighbors, or maybe you're *our* new neighbor. I'm Hua, and this is my wife, Margaret." Hua chuckled, her dimples spreading smile lines across her face. "Anyway, we brought you a gift basket and just wanted to welcome you to the neighborhood." Hua smiled while Margaret let go of the basket to shake Sarah's hand.

"Hey, girl. Hey, girl," Margaret cooed, handing the basket off to Sarah before leaning down to pet the tail-wagging pooch.

Sarah did all she could to muster up some semblance of social grace after being roused out of her reverie. Could she ever get some rest in this town?

Pulling herself together, she thought, *Okay, I can do this.*

"Hi, my name is Sarah Spellwood, and I'm pleased to meet you, Hua and Margaret," Sarah said, smiling sincerely. "Please, come in."

"We knew our neighbor, Michael, well. We were actually the ones who found him after we hadn't seen him for a few days," Margaret said sadly. "We own that greenhouse next door." Margaret smiled, tucking a strand of ebony hair behind her ear before pointing to the large roof next door that could barely be seen through the trees.

Stumbling a bit with the bulk of the produce basket, Sarah placed it on the couch after deciding that bringing it into the back room wouldn't be such a good idea. Until she had a chance to clean the house out thoroughly, she wasn't about to subject her guests to the dusty mess. That wouldn't be very neighborly. "Well, thank you. These look lovely," she said, gazing at the bright peppers, bunches of herbs, and bundles of carrots she could see just on the surface. Judging by the weight of the basket, there were doubtless other delectable-looking vegetables concealed beneath them as well.

"Michael always loved it when we brought the produce grown from our greenhouse to him." Hua chuckled. "Otherwise, he'd just never eat anything healthy. Pretty soon, we just started making the poor man meals every single week. Goodness knows he'd never made any himself . . . other than those awful microwave meals he was always eating. The stench of those things with their fake sauces!"

Margaret grinned mournfully. "We miss him so much. Please, know that if you ever need anything, my wife and I are just over there past the greenhouse. We loved Michael, and some of the most exciting times we had were when he would ask us for help with settling a dispute he was having. While we aren't lawyers, we do know a thing or two about how important a healthy environment is for our community."

"This place does need a lot of protecting, and that was Michael's forte," Hua said meaningfully.

"I won't promise that my work will need any dispute resolution, but thank you for the offer," Sarah added, moving out of Addie's way. Addie had decided to get in some pets from Hua as well. "I'm actually kind of taking a break from work for a while."

Hua playfully shook her head. "That's what we said when we left our old jobs in New York, but Witchland, despite being the peaceful place it is, always seems to bring us back to the work we're meant to do. You'll see. Wonderful and exciting things can happen in Witchland if you let them. Witchland has its own magic that infects most of the people who come here."

Sarah nodded slowly. "I used to visit here as a little girl. You're right about the magic here."

The women exchanged thrilled glances. "In fact, we heard you were a relative of Lativia Spellwood. How awesome," Margaret went on, looking almost . . . expectant?

Oh no, here it comes, Sarah thought to herself. *The Lativia Spellwood fan club. And what was that look between Hua and Margaret about?*

Sarah sighed behind her smile. "Yep, I am a Spellwood."

"Don't worry. We won't ask you to cast a spell," Hua teased. "I'm sure you get that a lot. We just are thrilled to have you here, especially after all that Michael told us about you, his star student at New York University Law!"

Sarah pretended to be modest, though she knew she had been his star student as well as his favorite. "He gives me entirely too much credit. He was quite the wonderful teacher." Then she realized that perhaps the two would have some answers to her many burning questions. "I find his death quite mysterious and odd. . . ."

Margaret abruptly rose from her kneeling position, leaving a disappointed Addie behind. "Oh, look at the time. We need to get going to the greenhouse and get the rest of the plants watered. But it was very nice to meet you, Sarah."

Sarah shook both women's hands, thanking them again before the pair left, and wheeled around to face the door into the dirty back room. If she was going to keep having visitors to this place, then it certainly needed to be cleaned up and made presentable. How could she possibly host clients here?

"Let's start organizing, Addie, and we can make this place something Michael would be proud of," she announced, hearing the dog whine in agreement. "But first let's go get my Beamer so I can get my stuff into this house."

After moving her car from where she had left it in the town square and parking it in front of the house, Sarah rolled up her sleeves and got down to work, thinking to herself, *Hmmm . . . Margaret and Hua are interesting. They sure didn't want to talk about Michael, did they? I wonder if they know something? Or suspect something, as I do? Being next door, they may have seen or heard something.* "And what did Hua mean by 'exciting things can happen in Witchland if you let them'? I guess we're going to find out, Addie."

CHAPTER SIX

"Ｗʜᴀᴛ ᴏɴ ᴇᴀʀᴛʜ ᴅᴏ ʏᴏᴜ ᴍᴇᴀɴ ʏᴏᴜ ᴍᴏᴠᴇᴅ ᴛᴏ Witchland?" Sarah's mother's voice grew shrill on the phone.

"Witchland?" Sarah heard her father pipe up in the background, undoubtedly from the recliner where he always lounged listening to records and reading dense old law books. Sarah could also picture her mother, messing with her houseplants or cooking something, the phone cradled between her ear and shoulder, dropping everything to give her husband an appalling look over Sarah's announcement.

"Yes," Sarah breathed calmly. She had expected this rejection, more or less. That was why she had put off the call home for a few days. "Michael left everything to me, and it seemed like a no-brainer to come here."

"Sarah, you had everything in New York! You had a life you could be proud of!" her mother chided her.

"Momma, I had nothing in New York," Sarah responded sorrowfully, feeling the full truth of her words deep in her heart.

Her mother was silent for a moment. Then she said gently, "I understand. Divorce rattles people."

"I also quit my job," Sarah added.

"What?!" both of her parents exclaimed. They were silent for a few minutes as Sarah explained why. Then her mother let out a long sigh. "As long as you're happy, Sarah. I trust you will still be working in Witchland? You can't let that law degree go to waste. You worked so hard for it."

"And I paid for so much of it," her father grumbled in the background.

"Of course. I am picking up where Michael left off, I guess," Sarah responded.

"Don't be getting into all that witchy mumbo jumbo up there," her father added. "You know how crazy that town can get." Having grown up in Witchland with the Spellwood name, her father had completely disowned anything to do with magic when he left for Columbia Law.

In many ways, Sarah was exactly like him.

"I won't. Trust me." Sarah laughed.

Her parents wished her luck and said they loved

her. When they said goodbye, she could still sense doubt and puzzlement in their voices. *Oh, well, they will just have to get used to this. Maybe I won't stay here forever, but how can I pass up this great house and an opportunity for a fresh start in a beautiful town where I was happy as a kid?*

"Okay," she muttered for the billionth time as she pulled out another folder, reminding herself of the organizational rules she had put in place. "Past clients and finished cases go in the gray filing cabinet, open cases go on the bookshelf by the door, and urgent meetings stay on the desk."

A few days had passed since John had shoved his way through her door and leveled his tacit threat. Those days had mostly been spent trying to turn Michael's unorganized mess in his office into something that resembled order. At least his client meeting room was now squeaky clean.

She had cleaned, scrubbed, wiped, and dusted the entire first floor of the house. Her efforts cast out the dust bunnies, removed the layers of dirt and grime from the floors and windows, and she had even attempted to take a crack at Michael's large stacks of files that seemed to be everywhere she turned.

So far, in spite of her best efforts, all she was able to do was to put a dent in the disorganization. Papers and folders were still stacked everywhere with almost no rhyme or reason to them. But if there was one thing that Sarah Spellwood did not do, it was give up, especially when her mentor was the man who had taught her to *never* quit. As she flipped through folder after folder and tried to decipher Michael's chicken-scratch handwriting to determine which of those three categories they belonged in, she tossed a glance at Addie, who was lounging on the carpet without a care in the world.

"Why is this so hard, Addie?" she asked, chuckling as Addie flopped onto her side to take in the noonday sun streaming through the window. "I wish I was more like you and could easily take any situation in stride—content no matter what was going on. How do you do it?" Sarah fondly watched her dog wiggle onto her back with legs sticking straight up in the air. "How can that position be comfortable?" She smiled before going back to the mess. "Maybe that's what was missing in New York . . . a dog. I love dogs. I love all animals."

While Michael was one of the greatest real estate lawyers in New York, an organizer he was not. Not by any means. His chicken-scratch handwriting, which got even more unintelligible the more rushed he was, made it all the more difficult to decipher the order in the mess. Judging by the quality of the handwriting she had seen so far, he'd been rushed while working on at least three-quarters of his cases.

The directions he had left himself weren't helping her out either, as most folders or papers simply had something along the lines of 'see paper in other folder' at the bottom, which did nothing to help her.

"I'm up to my elbows in documents, sticky notes, and hastily scrawled messages on notepads," Sarah said loudly while pushing her curls away from her eyes.

She looked at the three piles that were supposed to help her sort out this mess. None of them seemed to be getting any bigger. Sarah confided with Addie, as she pulled another stack of papers toward her and began to flip through them, "Will I ever get through this?"

Looking up, she locked her eyes on the photo Michael had tacked to the wall just above his desk—one of the two that included both of them. It was that special day she had graduated and received her law degree. They were standing on stage together and smiling as if the world was all about them. "For that day, maybe it was," Sarah said out loud while tears made the mess in front of her a blur of manila.

As Sarah paused to look around, she noticed that the only things in the room that were even remotely organized were his photos. All of them were standing in frames around his office, carefully tacked to the walls, or neatly stuck onto the fridge upstairs. The photos and his hiking gear hanging neatly in his closet were the only things he had organized with purpose.

That man always let his backroom professional life get into shambles but would make his personal life and space for his clients as neat as a library, Sarah thought, chuckling a bit as she flipped through another folder, breathing a sigh of relief as she finally found an old finished case she could stuff into the filing cabinet.

At least she'd learned from his bad habits. Her desk back at her old law firm was immaculate and organized, as was her computer. It had to be in order to find anything. It was also company policy to file a certain way.

Despite promising to mentor him on a desktop's use, Michael had never really gotten behind the whole 'computer thing.' He preferred to have all his cases and data splayed out where he could see them, which obviously led to the mess she had spent the past three days trying to sift through.

"Computers are too confounding and impersonal," Michael had always said. He even balked at the idea of a website to advertise his services, even though Sarah had offered to design it for him.

Finally, after another half hour of squinting at his handwriting and placing the few files she had managed to organize away, she stretched and stood up. Maybe Addie had the right idea; she just needed some sun on her skin and then she could return to the mess with even greater vigor and fresh eyes. Such a strategy had worked in the past, after all, when she left stress behind in the office to work it out in the gym.

"Addie? You wanna go for a walk?" she asked, watching the dog leap up and wag her tail before bounding for the door with her tongue lolling out. "Guess that's a yes, huh?"

She walked over to the door and opened it, letting the dog out before locking the office and heading outside. She almost turned back to grab Addie's leash but thought better of it when she saw the dog patiently stop and wait for her to catch up. Addie was incredibly smart, so maybe she didn't need a leash for a walk. She also knew this area, and it wasn't like there were cars and crowds and other dangers all around, so no leash it was.

Walking through the small town, Sarah soaked up the sun beating down on her skin as Addie trotted obediently by her side. Inhaling and then exhaling the fresh air, she walked down the street with a noticeable spring in her step. Her brain was already making mental notes of where everything was. A few more trips through the town and she'd have everything perfectly memorized.

The city she had lived in for so long certainly had its pluses, but it sure gave her the sense she was a small, insignificant speck in a mire of people who didn't care if she lived or died. She'd heard cities described as concrete jungles, and now that she was out of the city, that analogy seemed very accurate. The tall buildings, the noxious smoke of a million cars, and the pressing crush of people rushing this way and that had always left her feeling overwhelmed. It was as if New York City was a concrete cage where she had spent a lot of her life trapped along with the rest of the city rats, only given the illusion of freedom from time to time.

Witchland was so different and truly freeing, she realized. Unlike the tall steel buildings, the massive trees hemming in the town from all directions didn't trigger feelings of claustrophobia.

Crossing the town square, she came upon a hand-carved, artfully designed footbridge across the river. On the other side lay the forest, and a series of trail-heads heading into the trees. The forest covered the side of a mountain, whose peak was veiled in mist. A sign declared it to be the Mount Katribus Wilderness Area, a three-hundred-acre conservation area where motor vehicles were only allowed on designated roads that led to parking and littering was strictly prohib-ited. A little map showed the trail system and the loca-tion of the hunting lodge, both of which Sarah had heard were internationally renowned, attracting hunters and hikers from all over the world. *Why not go hiking and clear my mind a bit?* she thought and laughed to herself. *It's a good thing I took off my*

Jimmy Choos. These tennis shoes are so much more comfy, anyway. It feels like my feet can actually breathe!

"Yeah, the next to go is that crazy lipstick you are wearing," said the short woman with the slouchy pointed hat that Sarah had encountered on her first day in Witchland. She was riding her bicycle past the startled Sarah.

"What's wrong with wearing lipstick?" yelled Sarah, too late for the passing woman to hear. *And how did she know I was thinking about my city shoes?*

"Geez Louise! No privacy here! Come on, Addie," she called, tapping her knees and watching Addie run right to her. "Let's go for a hike."

As she walked up to the bridge and toward the bordering forest, she spotted her two neighbors coming out of the market across the way, bearing a huge loaf of fresh-baked French bread.

"Hey, Margaret and Hua." She smiled, feeling totally happy to see them this time. Sarah walked over as Addie wove around her legs, a little upset at the interruption.

"Hello, Sarah." Margaret beamed, reaching over to give Sarah a hug. "Out for some fresh air, I see? Gorgeous day we have here. We just picked up some things for dinner. You should check out the market after you settle in. Great vegan options here!"

Sarah grinned. "Glad to hear that! You're vegan, too?"

"Of course." Both women nodded enthusiastically.

"Addie and I have been cleaning Michael's office all morning, and after all that work we needed a break. Whew," Sarah teased, seeing Hua crack a smile. "He's got so many papers in his office that I'm surprised the forest isn't smaller because of it."

"I know. He very rarely let us into his office, but whenever we stopped by, we could certainly see the mess. I can only imagine what the chaos looks like up close. Did you find anything of interest?" Hua chuckled inquiringly. "Let us know if you need any help. We're pretty good at organizing."

"Got it." Sarah smiled. "Well, we'll see you guys later. Addie and I are going to explore one of the trails and maybe hike to the top of Mount Katribus."

"Stay on the marked trails if you do, since the unmarked trails are not on the maps. You won't likely be rescued if you do get lost by going too deep into the forest. As long as you stay on the trails with stones or marked trees, you'll be fine," Hua warned, her gaze surprisingly serious as she looked up at the mountain before her face cracked, and she started laughing.

Margaret smiled and laid a hand on her shoulder. "Did we have you worried for a second? That's a little joke we like to play on all the newcomers here. You'll be rescued, but it's easier to stick to the marked trails simply because people haven't gotten around to finishing the entire project."

"There's also a camera at the head of the trails that's triggered when someone walks under the entrance, and when they walk out. That way, we have a tally of who's in the forest and who hasn't come out yet," Hua explained.

"Got it," Sarah answered, laughing a bit at herself about the kindness and overconcern of Witchlanders before she waved goodbye and crossed over the bridge toward the kiosk that displayed a massive map of the forest where the trails began.

"Shall we take the Witchland Forest Loop, Addie?" she asked after gazing at the map for a second, watching Addie chase her tail as an answer. "Good enough for me. Let's go, girl!"

CHAPTER SEVEN

Walking up the trail, Sarah kept her eyes on the bright yellow trail markers for the Witchland Forest Loop. "I'll be danged if I let Hua's kidding get the best of me. Yet, what did she mean, did I find anything interesting?" she said. Her attention soon wandered, however, as she began to allow herself to become mesmerized by the forest's beauty. Red toadstools with little white dots on their caps looked like faery homes; the trees looked ancient, with rugged moss turning their trunks green, and sunlight dappling the forest floor between their leaves. She observed little holes hidden among tree roots or in whorls in the trunks and mused about what animals called them home, how their homes looked inside. The sights, sounds, and fresh air delighted her senses, making her feel millions of miles away from files and clients and divorce and everything else routinely on her mind. She felt like a little girl again.

Finding another yellow marker, she followed the path to the right and giggled as Addie tried to chase a squirrel scampering up a tree.

Birds were flitting around the treetops, chirping and singing to one another. The rich undergrowth filled her nostrils with the earthy aroma of ferns and moss, and the gentle breeze wafted scents of sweet-smelling wildflowers and damp moss across her path. She even saw a raccoon rummaging around the roots of a big oak on her left before it vanished into the undergrowth. Sarah took a deep breath. "This whole experience is quite peaceful and calming. It is completely unlike my walks in the noisy city, choking on exhaust fumes, rushing and elbowing my way through large crowds to make sure I was on time for the next court case. Phew, I am so glad that part of my life is over."

The new leg of the trail, or at least what was left of it, had been largely reclaimed by grasses and wildflowers. She had to leap over the branches and skip over small streams. Addie agilely leaped over the obstacles and ended up with muddy paws and sticks in her long, golden fur.

"Addie, let's go this way . . . stay with me!" Sarah called.

Around the next bend, the trail widened, and once

Sarah got clear of the brambles, her steps became faster as she walked through the twists and turns. The dirt path occasionally shifted under her feet as loose stones and gravel rolled out from under her shoes with each step. She ascended the lower slopes of Mount Katribus. "Why is this part of the trail not maintained as well as the rest?" she mused aloud.

Deep in thought and not paying close attention to her footing, she skidded over a root and landed square on her butt. There, before her in the mud, was the print of a large animal. The print was clearly outlined by ridges of dried earth.

"What's this?" she asked Addie, while looking closer at tracks that looked like ice cream cones. "I wonder if these are tracks from the lynx I read about in Michael's files?" Instinctively, she placed her hand in the track, which fit remarkably well. All of a sudden, she felt a tingling sensation through her fingers that startled her.

Ooooh . . . that's weird. She pulled her hand back quickly and looked at her palm. That track actually felt warm, and what was that tingling sensation all about?

As she sat there, she recited in her mind what she had read about lynx among Michael's files: "Mostly solitary cats, medium size, non-aggressive, hunts snowshoe hare, lives in large, unfragmented tracts of land dominated by conifers."

Mmmmm, I wonder . . .

Getting up and brushing her hands free of dirt, she regained her footing on the upward climb. For the first time in a long while, she just walked, not having to worry about being at the firm on time and not having to apologize to the crowd she was forcing her way through. It was peaceful, soothing, and calming just to be out in nature for a little bit. Her eyes glanced up at the clouds, trying to imagine what shapes they looked like.

"Look at that, Addie. Some of them look like birds and others like elephants or whales, all lazily moving across the sky. Now, that one there, see it? It looks like a diminutive little creature with wings—kinda faerylike."

After about twenty minutes, Sarah stopped moving to sit down on a large rock, where she looked over at a smiling Addie. Sarah scratched her behind her ears before turning back to look at the town coming into view through the trees. Although most of it was hidden by the massive trunks of oak and pine trees, bits of rooftops, steeples, and the lumber mill could be seen through the hanging branches and leaves. From what she could see of the town, it looked impossibly small from where she was.

"New York never made me feel this way before. This town is small enough that I feel like I can make a difference and not just fight cases that line someone else's pockets. I can help people. I can be my own boss, so no guilt, shaming, or harassment here." She smiled. "We'll do good for this town, right, Addie? Addie?"

Looking down at the empty patch of dirt where the dog had just been sitting enjoying an ear scratching, Sarah turned around in a panic, her heart rising into her throat as she looked from side to side.

"Addie? Addie! Come here, girl!" she cried, hoping the dog had simply gone to check out a chipmunk hole or something and was nearby. When she didn't hear Addie's collar jingle or see her golden fur appearing through the foliage crowding the trail, Sarah began to run down the path, unsure where her dog had gone and doubtful which way to go. Moving in any direction was far better than standing still.

CHAPTER EIGHT

"Addie! Where are you? Here, girl." She called Addie's name using whatever air she could suck from her lungs when she wasn't running down the path, peering through the green leaves and branches to try and catch a glimpse of her dog's fur.

Addie is the only thing of Michael's I have left. She is something I simply cannot lose.

The thought of losing Addie freaked her out so much she came to a full stop as she realized it didn't matter how Michael had died; he'd come back from the grave and haunt her forever if she let his dog come to harm. That much she knew.

"Over here!" a voice called from her left, and she exhaled slowly in relief before running again in its direction. The person was off the path, but as long as whoever it was had her dog, being off the path didn't matter. Maybe they could give her directions back. Pushing her way through the branches and underbrush, she ignored the scrape of branches and brambles across her skin. Her strength, born of desperation and worry about her dog, shoved everything else aside.

She broke out into a small clearing and took a deep breath when she saw Addie sitting on the ground at the base of a tree. She brushed off the brambles and stray leaves stuck to her clothes and crazy red curls as she tried to calm her racing heart.

"Addie, thank goodness you're okay," Sarah breathed, kneeling down to squeeze the dog in a tight bear hug as Addie licked at Sarah's face. Her fingers caressed the dog's fur as Addie nuzzled in. Sarah wasn't alone anymore, and Addie was safe.

After the quick reunion, Sarah looked up, noticing there was no one around to thank. She saw no footprints, and her ears didn't pick up any sounds of someone moving through the undergrowth.

Where was Addie's rescuer? Where was the person who called out?

She surveyed the area around them and saw it was relatively clear. Unless that person had managed to dart behind one of the trees and was a phenomenal hider, there was no sign of anyone or anything.

"Who called me here?" she asked out loud, hearing her voice ominously echo off the trees as she took a deep breath. "Show yourself." She mustered her strength, although deep down, she was beginning to fear her own defenselessness, and she was acutely aware of the fact she was well off the trail in the middle of the deep, seemingly dark woods.

At least she knew someone would come looking for her eventually, but even that didn't give her much peace of mind as the trees creaked around her.

"*I did!*" the voice called again, this time from below her, and as she looked down, she saw Addie staring up at her with a wagging tail.

Did she just . . . speak? Okay, that was not possible. Calm down, Sarah, she thought to herself, taking slow, deep breaths as she squeezed her hands together. A memory of the talking goat in Aunt Beth's field flitted through her mind, but she shoved it aside. *It's not possible!*

"Addie?" Sarah whispered, as her knees gave out beneath her, and she found herself sitting on a bed of moss. Sarah desperately tried to ground herself as Addie made eye contact.

"*Yes, I can speak, and I am your familiar. I'm here to guide you.*"

"Guide me?" Sarah repeated dumbly.

"*I am here to help you make decisions and to protect you. What you need to do is just listen to me. Right now,*

I need to show you something very important," Addie explained.

Sarah's hand reached out to grip the closest solid object just to reassure herself that she was awake, present, and hearing what she thought she was hearing. Even though her legs had turned to jelly, her mind still sought a logical conclusion as to why this was happening. Maybe this was a dream, or she was sick, or this was all some kind of prank that every newbie to Witchland experienced somehow. Or maybe . . . her witchy powers were getting stronger again because she now lived in Witchland. Her childhood of talking to animals and trees, levitating objects with her mind, and dreaming things before they happened had been real, but it had all happened here in Witchland. When returning to her home in Albany or visiting Witchland as a child, weird things still happened on occasion, but not very often. Maybe there was a reason why; maybe there was an element of truth in what Hua had said: "Good things happen here if you let them."

Or, alternatively, Sarah was just insane.

"N—no, you can't . . . really . . . speak," Sarah finally gasped when she got her breath back, scooting back as Addie came closer. "Can you? Is this real?"

Even if this was somehow real, how did Addie get this ability? Did Michael know? Why didn't Addie ever speak before?

"*Yes, I can!*" responded Addie, her tail wagging as she began to bounce around. "*I need to show you something, though.*"

Sarah shook her head, trying to wake up from this improbable daydream about Michael's dog actually speaking to her. As she did so, she leaned back against what seemed like a tree, yet upon hearing it creak and feeling it bend under her weight, she sprang up and looked around. It was not a tree at all but an old, weathered fencepost, supporting a sagging wooden fence that stretched all the way across the clearing until it disappeared back into the forest line. It was completely overgrown with lichens and mosses that had found homes on the rotting wood, with weeds and vines wrapped around the posts. The sheer overgrowth of plant life probably made sure the fence was still standing, even though it was mostly rotten now.

She gently touched the rotting wood, feeling like it would crumble in her hands if she put the slightest pressure on it. It seemed to be decades old and completely left to the elements.

Why would there be a wooden fence here and not a stone one? she wondered, stopping herself from turning toward Addie to ask that very question. Then she noticed a little historical plaque, mostly swallowed in vines. She pushed the vines aside and read that the fence surrounded the site of the official home of Lativia

Spellwood. After Lativia's passing, the house had become the official Wolf Coven Lodge, where her followers continued to practice her magic. The stone lodge had been completely destroyed by witch hunters in 1936 and then the stones had been carted off or scattered by vandals over the years since, leaving no trace of the witch's former abode. But the fence had been maintained for years as a relic of a long-past era, until finally state funding stopped including its care. This site had once seen many tourists, but that had waned with increased interest in the second version of the Wolf Coven Lodge, which had been built inside Witchland and converted into a museum.

"Follow the fence line," Addie told her. "There is something very important for you to see at the end of this fence."

Sarah glanced back at Addie, extremely perplexed. "Did I fall and hit my head?" she demanded.

"No." Addie grinned, wagging her tail eagerly. *"You are saner and more aware than you have been in years. You just need to listen to me! Follow the fence!"*

The fence didn't look like it was protecting anything of importance, and she doubted it was a boundary fence. Maybe it belonged to some old, overgrown home from decades earlier, or given the town's history, it could be a remnant from the heyday of the sawmill during the last century.

Her suppositions weren't enough to settle her rampant curiosity. Sarah began to walk toward the other end of the fence. *If I find where it ended, I might get some answers.* The fence ended a few feet to her left, but disappeared into the trees to her right, so that's where she walked, Addie hot on her heels.

"*Sarah!*" Addie barked, moving toward her and pointing behind Sarah with her nose. "*You're going the right way! Keep walking! Just a little farther now.*"

"How is this happening?" Sarah muttered. This reminded her so much of her days on Aunt Beth's farm, getting lost in the forest with the goat whom she had named Norman. Norman would tell her where to find berries that she could safely eat, or where to hide from rain. He often would chat with her as if she were a friend, telling her that he was her familiar as well. Was this all just a memory of childhood, or a dream?

As her hands pushed aside the lower branches above the old fence, she wrinkled her nose at the resinous smell. Under the moss was a pine cone moving on its own. "Hmm . . . that's odd. Must be some kind of weird animal or worm or something in it," she posed.

She looked up into the pine trees towering over her, and her eyes picked out the fresh crop of pine cones still growing on the branches. She worried one might torpedo down onto her head, since more pine cones littered the ground as she kept moving deeper into the grove. After a few more steps, the fence ended as abruptly as it had begun. The last post was surrounded by ferns, covered in moss, with next to nothing remarkable about it aside from the abundance of pine cones collected on the ground all around the area.

"What is it that you're showing me?" she asked Addie, deciding to play along with whatever this whole thing was.

"Pick up one of the pine cones," Addie urged her.

She picked up one of the cones and examined it. Nothing seemed remarkable about it, beyond a few squirrel teeth marks on some of the scales. She set it back down and leaned forward, reaching for another one, before it began to roll away from her.

What the heck? A moving pine cone?

Her fingers moved to grab the pine cone, only for it to wiggle next to another one, and that pine cone began to wiggle, then one of the pine cones at her feet began to wiggle as well.

"This is *not* normal," expressed Sarah. Then she gasped and began to back up as more pine cones began to join in, vibrating and buzzing. Some of them simply moved from side to side, while others jumped up and down as if they were in the pine cone Olympics, doing flips and springing up off the ground.

She was completely surrounded by these crazed pine cones as she backed up against a tree in mild shock. She started as her hands touched the massive buttress of wood behind her.

"Ad—d—die, what's happening?" Sarah muttered as she shook herself to try and clear her mind.

The pine cones suddenly filled the air with crackling and shuffling sounds. And then, all at once, they all stopped moving without warning, leaving her alone with an eerie silence as Addie sat down at her feet.

Miraculously, out of the pine cones poured dozens upon dozens of small creatures, each about an inch tall. She couldn't tell much more than that, since they completely covered the ground and leaves in a writhing brown mass. There were probably a couple hundred of them, all moving with a purpose only they knew about as they climbed out, one by one, from each of the wiggling pine cones. Sarah briefly turned around to plan an escape route when she stopped at Addie's bark.

"Don't be afraid of them! They're friendly!" she barked, sitting perfectly still as the creatures squirmed and streamed all around her.

"Friendly? Are you kidding me?" Sarah recoiled in shock, keeping herself as still as possible while scores of the little creatures ran toward the base of one of the fenceposts. She wanted to run away, but she was scared to trample the tiny beings underfoot.

"Oh, my stars! What's going on now?" she asked, exasperated but also mildly frightened.

She could not believe what she was seeing as she watched several of them climb on top of one another, while others used themselves as platforms, and some flew into the air itself with tiny wings on their backs. It looked rather chaotic with the creatures flying or climbing every which way. But soon, the chaos neatened into a perfect pyramid of the brown creatures. The creature on the pinnacle stood smack in front of her face. Now Sarah could see details of the creatures start to clarify and crystallize, and she gasped yet again. The creature on the pinnacle stared at her with a haughty expression and hands on her hips.

With a squint and several deep breaths to calm her racing heart, she examined the odd being, wishing she'd thought to bring her glasses. It looked like a tiny human, with brown skin, large three-toed feet, and tiny transparent wings poking out of its back. It was wearing a scrap of ripped clothing and seemed to be a female because of its long, fine, purple hair tied back in a braid and adorned with a crown of tiny flowers and moss. She stared up at Sarah, as if indignant about her presence.

"Why have you come to Witchland Forest and disturbed us?" the creature demanded in a squeaky voice—the sound surprisingly audible despite the creature's size. She gazed at Sarah intensely with her golden eyes, her hands still on her hips. "You humans are not supposed to be here. Only *special* people are allowed to visit our fence."

"*Clover Figcreek, Sarah is a friend,*" Addie interrupted, wagging her tail. "*She knew Michael.*"

"You know Michael?" Clover Figcreek inquired, her tiny eyes burning into Sarah's with ferocity, demanding an answer to her question. Her slender-fingered hands gripped the air in front of Sarah. As if on cue, the mass of creatures moved her closer to Sarah's face. *How did they know how to do that?* thought Sarah, shaking a bit from this latest acrobatic escapade.

"*Clover Figcreek, this is the one Michael was telling you about! His prodigy, who would come help us once he passed!*" Addie went on.

Clover Figcreek peered more closely at Sarah. "And you're just getting here now? How come I haven't met you yet?"

"Well . . . I just came here," Sarah said apologetically.

"*I led her out here today, but I couldn't make her hear me before,*" Addie added.

"Michael is dead. He fell down his stairs," Sarah continued remorsefully, the words springing unbidden to her lips before she could stop them, her brain still trying to rationalize all that had happened and was still happening. She sure as hell wasn't going to tell these creatures about the note written on scrap paper.

"Eeeeeeeowwwww! Don't speak of his death! We miss him!" Clover Figcreek let out a loud and piercing wail—a wail echoed by the rest of her people as her chocolate skin began to turn a dark shade of blue and tears welled up in her eyes. The pyramid of creatures below her began to turn blue and wail as well. Sarah could almost feel their sadness as she took a deep breath.

"I'm sorry to interrupt your grieving, er—Ms. Figcreek, but how did you know Michael?" she asked, perplexed that supposedly these tiny individuals knew about her existence already. Stepping back a bit as the creatures' tears formed a small puddle at her feet, she struggled to make herself heard over the sounds. "And who *are* you, anyway?" Noticing one of the small creatures dangling by its toes swinging in the breeze.

"They're the Leekins," Addie explained. *"Protectors of this forest, all the creatures that live in it, and the town of Witchland. You didn't think that all those flowers were kept up by humans, did you? These forest faeries help the flowers, the animals, and the forest grow while keeping all of nature safe. Thankfully, the humans living in Witchland respect nature and allow the Leekins to do their work. Not many people know*

they exist, but now you do, and Michael did, too. Michael discovered them when he came here, but he always had strong intuition."

Sarah nodded. Michael had often tried to bring up things—premonitions, ghost encounters, his belief in magic—but Sarah had always cut him off and reminded him to focus on the practical. Swallowing her disbelief, she looked down at her dog and said, "All right, so then how can you talk like a human?"

"They saved me when I was a puppy," Addie yipped, her face twisting into something like a frown. *"I didn't have a home before Michael, but I lived in the town's back alleys and survived on garbage. Then, one day, a storm came, and I was hit on my head by a tree branch while I was out exploring the woods. When I woke up, the Leekins were all around me, and somehow I could understand them. They said they knew a very kind man who would take me in. They introduced me to Michael, and he adopted me."* Her tail began to wag as the story reached its happy conclusion, her eyes shining up at Sarah.

"While I was near the Leekins, I could understand Michael and could even speak to him in human language. Then, when he took me home, I couldn't speak to him, but I could still understand him. The Leekins put a spell on him so that he could understand me when they saw how sad he was to not be able to."

"So when you're near the Leekins, you can speak with people?" Sarah asked, reasoning out how Addie could speak. "And they have to put a spell on people to keep hearing you speaking like a human?"

Addie nodded.

Sarah continued, "Why do these . . . Leekins care so much about Michael?"

Clover Figcreek interjected, "He protected us and all the forest creatures, especially the lynx, from the bad machines. Big, big, bad machines that shoot smoke and break trees where we live. He came to this land to be our voice in the human world, and now that he is gone, we need you to help us." Clover Figcreek blotted her tears dry as her skin began to fade back to its chocolate color. "Or the machines will come and destroy the home we have protected for generations."

"Well," Sarah admitted, "I do have his notes and knowledge." Then she added, "I did believe in everything he did," thinking back to her conversation with John and his crusade for progress. Plus, from those she had met and what she had seen of the town, most of the people seemed to enjoy having the forest nearby. They took pride in the fact all of their goods were handmade from carefully selected trees. In general, they were opposed to the developers' plans. Even if all this fantasy stuff was some crazy hallucination brought on by the stress of having to move and deal with her mentor's murder, it certainly seemed like a good idea to support the town, keep the forest the way it is, and help an essential predator survive in the region.

"But why can't you just move to another forest, or even use your magic to scare off the people in the machines?" Sarah asked, playing along with this improbable hallucination.

"Move to another forest?!" Clover Figcreek shouted. "You humans—you think that just because you move to a different house, the concept of home will travel with you. This forest is our home and has been for centuries. We cannot possibly move." The Leekin placed her hands on her hips, jutting her chin out as she spoke. "We are here because of Lativia Spellwood: the greatest forest witch of all time."

Sarah shrank back from the name.

"Yes, I know who you are to her. The question is, is she anything to you?" Clover Figcreek demanded. "You seem terribly ordinary."

Sarah felt stung. "I'm not ordinary!"

"We need a strong witch to protect us. You see, we don't like many humans. We scared the destructive humans away from our woods for many years, keeping them away while they still believed in magic and ghosts. They said this forest was haunted, that strange things happened here. Now that they do not believe in such things, they are not so scared. The developers are after our land and all the creatures within, including the lynx. And the bad man doing their bidding is the Hunter." Clover Figcreek shuddered, her skin and the skin of those beneath her instantly turning white with fear.

"Aiee! The Hunter!" several of the Leekins cried.

This kicked off another round of screaming and wailing as Addie shivered, pressing herself against Sarah. *"The Hunter is a bad man. He wants to kill the lynx and every other animal to put them on his wall,"* Addie growled, understandably terrified.

Sarah reached down to pet Addie, soothing her, as Clover Figcreek cried out, "The Hunter comes armed with blades, noisemakers, and silver. Aieee!" Sarah watched the tiny faeries shudder in fear, feeling the smallest twinge of pity for them. Such odd creatures they were that they couldn't possibly be real, yet their emotions were tangible, and they seemed like extensions of the forest themselves.

"If the development is permitted, then he will hunt down the lynx and destroy the forest. Then we will have no home, the town will crumble, and all that we've worked for will be for nothing," Clover Figcreek cried, turning to look at Sarah. "You must help us. You know what Michael knew, and you can take his place in fighting for us."

All at once, the creatures began to beg her, the

pyramid quivering and looking as though it would buckle under the weight of the shivering creatures. The noise was deafening as Addie looked up at Sarah, whimpering in distress, her tail tucked between her legs.

"Okay, okay, okay, I will," Sarah cried, raising her hands as she tried to get these creatures to stop crying. Geez, these figments of her imagination were annoying. "But you need to help me get back to Witchland."

"Good." Clover Figcreek clapped her tiny hands and smiled, the crying and begging instantly coming to a stop. Then she raised her hand and whistled, sending three more tiny Leekins rushing out from the undergrowth.

The trio was holding a bottle up to Sarah, which contained a gold swirling liquid inside of it. The glass was about the length of her index finger. Sarah smiled as she took the bottle and tucked it into her pocket, confident it would be gone the moment she woke up from this crazy dream.

"Take this to help you, but do not drink it until it is time; we shall give you the same gift we gave Michael, and Addie will lead you back to town. Thank you, Sarah. Thank you for agreeing to defend us and to find out what really happened to Michael." Clover Figcreek clapped.

Sarah nodded thanks as the two Leekins who were

carrying Clover Figcreek let her down. Then, almost faster than the eye could see, the pyramid of Leekins instantly dispersed, layer by layer, with the creatures rushing back into their pine cones or down into the undergrowth. In a few seconds, they were gone, and Addie licked Sarah's hand.

"Let's go back home," Addie prompted her gently. *"I know the way by heart. Michael often came here with me to confer with the Leekins."*

As Sarah followed her dog out of the forest, past the fence, and back onto the trail, she smiled as Addie began to bark again. Nothing out of the ordinary, and nothing impossible about that bark. She was going to protect the forest because Michael wanted her to, as if it was his dying wish, not because some magical faeries that didn't and couldn't exist told her to.

Her eyes looked down along the path, and after seeing another carpet of pine cones on the ground, she shook her head. *Just ordinary pine cones and undergrowth. Nothing ridiculous here at all.*

She exited the forest and walked back into the town with Addie prancing by her side. As Sarah moved through the quaint town and nodded to the people, she reveled in what an odd dream she just had. She assumed she had fallen asleep in the forest and was now awake.

But when she reached Michael's, she felt something tiny and hard in her pocket. She pulled it out and felt faint when she recognized the gold swirling liquid inside the tiny bottle and put it on her nightstand. Addie looked at her, wagging her tail, and Sarah just knew she was talking.

CHAPTER NINE

When Sarah arrived back at Michael's office and closed the door, she watched Addie bolt toward her food bowl like a perfectly normal dog, devouring her food with large, gulping bites.

Sarah laughed. "I'm glad to see you have a normal appetite, Addie. I must remember to pick up some more ingredients when I head into town so I can make you more food. It seems like you're going to need it. I think I remember seeing the recipe somewhere in the kitchen."

Futzing around Michael's kitchen almost brought Sarah to tears again as memories of him punctuated her thoughts. *Oh, this is ridiculous—my emotions are on a roller-coaster ride.*

She had a tough time keeping it together while rummaging through the drawers to find Addie's food list. There were so many reminders of her mentor, from his favorite coffee mug to the kitschy kitchen witch she bought him a long time ago. "Ha—maybe this is a relative of mine." She giggled to give her heart a break from the sorrow, something Michael would have approved of. "Ah, here is that list, and it even has the recipe on it. Hmmm, looks good."

Returning to the never-ending task of organizing the office, she smiled as she came across a file with a large red "Current case" sticker on front. She was pleased to see he had occasionally used the sticker system she had taught him earlier, mostly in a vain attempt to help him get organized. It certainly was the easiest way to notice a file in the large pile. The cover sheet made her heart skip a beat, though, when she noticed that it entailed John Gonforth and an out-of-town development group.

Opening the file, a slip of paper drifted to the floor. Addie scampered toward the paper, picked it up in her mouth, and rested her head on Sarah's lap.

"Michael had apparently been working this case long before he died," Sarah lamented while staring at the large red 'Current Case' sticker on the front of the folder in her hands. "But what do you have here, Addie? Another piece of paper?"

She took the paper from Addie's mouth and wiped the slobber on her designer jeans, lamenting, "Geez, I would never have done this if I was still in Manhattan. Four-hundred-dollar jeans with a coat of dog slime . . . never." Bringing it up to her face so she could decipher Michael's chicken scratch, she read:

Make sure I get my will, key, and cover letter in place for Sarah just in case something happens to me.

"Addie, this doesn't look good," Sarah remarked. "Oh, right . . . you can't understand a word I am saying . . . regardless, this is not good."

Thinking about her recent discovery and not sure who she could talk to in the town who would take her seriously, she mused about whether or not Eli the Handsome Cop would want to see this. Surely it was evidence, right? Clearly, Michael feared for his life. And his fear seemed to have to do with this case.

"Michael was right when he called John Gonforth a terrible man," she muttered to herself, thankful that Addie didn't show any signs of acknowledging her thoughts, because she knew Addie couldn't talk or understand any human words other than a few, like 'food,' 'walk,' and 'come.' Right?

Based on Michael's file notes, it appeared that John was a man who would certainly do cutthroat things to win a court case. Witnesses would disappear, evidence would go missing, and professionals who would testify for the defense would suddenly refuse to talk or have scheduling conflicts. Although it couldn't be proven,

Michael felt that John had something to do with every single "anomaly" during the hearings of this case.

Hmmm, I wonder if John had anything to do with Michael's death? Sarah deliberated. The murdered witnesses made her blood run cold.

Court dockets showed that John was also a notorious cross-examiner on the stand, outright treating victims as hostile witnesses to get what he wanted. His questions were always designed to get inside someone's head, get them confused and emotional, and then exploit that weakness to its full extent. John thought nothing of using their exasperated outbursts as proof they were incompetent. *Geez, what a creep this guy is, and certainly a formidable enemy to go up against in court,* thought Sarah.

The developers John Gonforth was representing, B & M Real Estate, weren't much better, as they had apparently done this all before—taken small towns with few environmental regulations and bulldozed their land. After they flattened the land, they'd turn former forest and habitat into fancy high-rise commercial or residential buildings, and charge mucho bucks for profit-seeking individuals to rent or lease the spaces. The profits they reaped around the U.S. were astronomical.

On top of that, Michael seemed particularly concerned with the man that B & M Real Estate had hired to conduct their initial environmental impact evaluation. The man, Dismas Lorian, was a notorious trophy hunter with more than a few poaching and illegal trapping citations by Game and Fish from all over the nation. Dismas had proudly displayed the kills from his latest African safari on Facebook, and Michael had printed the pictures. It was clear Michael was building a case against this man's reputation as a wildlife consultant. "Why is he saying there is no lynx here?" Michael scrawled on the margin of the report Dismas Lorian had produced, which claimed the forest was devoid of the endangered species.

"This is despicable, completely and utterly despicable," she pronounced. She felt a sense of pride for Michael well up in her chest as she read his notes on how he tried to stop this obliteration. The idea of the lovely forest turning into some condos or hotel hurt her. Fantasy-Leekin-fueled hallucination or not, she was going to take this case and finish what Michael had started. That determination was real, and it caused her to break out into a smile of steely resolve before she closed the folder.

She put the file down on the desk and walked upstairs toward the bed, climbing under the covers without even taking off her clothes as Addie leaped onto the bed and curled up at her feet. Just like a regular dog would do, not one that could talk.

"All I need is a good night's sleep. Tomorrow, I can start working on this very real environmental case that is standing before me, instead of delving into mythic tales with talking faeries and dogs," she decided. "I am going to save the town, save the lynx, and figure out how Michael really died, but the make-believe Leekins aren't going to be on the agenda."

These were Sarah's last words as she began to float off into sleep.

Rolling onto her stomach, however, she groaned as something nagged at her. She reached towards the nightstand beside the bed, expecting to brush bare wood. But her fingertips felt the bottle the Leekins had given her, and her mouth fell open with shock. She bolted upright and stared at it. "It's still real," she mumbled aloud.

Addie whined and wagged her tail. Her eyes seemed to be saying, "See?"

Flopping back down and rolling back over, Sarah's mind spun wildly as she closed her eyes and struggled to get back to sleep. The bottle would disappear and be gone by morning, right?

CHAPTER TEN

The next day, Sarah woke up with a start and completely forgot about the little vial on the nightstand. She promptly dove right into work, foregoing breakfast. For the next few days, she tackled Michael's case against John and his developers.

Finding all of Michael's pertinent files on the case was the easy part because most of them were on the tops of the many messy piles she had already sorted through. It was the analysis of all the data associated with the case that proved to be the challenge. Her mind was strained to the limit trying to find the threads of legal defense that Michael was pursuing against the developers to keep them from being able to purchase the Witchland Forest from the town's government.

Thankfully, Michael's train of thought, unlike the man himself, was relatively easy to follow. She quickly latched on to his 'theme.' Michael saw cases as stories to be told to a judge, jury, or opponent. It was his story against his opponent's, and like every good writer, he had a theme for each case. The purpose of his themes were to emotionally sway everyone in court and empower them to make the right decision. He liked to build people up and call on their pride, intelligence, or good nature. Crafting a story with emotional components was always something crooked lawyers and developers never thought about, mostly because they were so focused on money, deception, and manipulating the minds of honest people with fear. Michael's proposed theme this time was fairly simple: appeal to the town's pride in itself and the common sense of its good, upstanding citizens. As she read through Michael's files, it was easy for her to find data to support this theme and connect all the dots to tell a convincing story.

There were forms and permit applications and all that bureaucratic matter, but the developers had all that and more. They were masters of facts and forms, yet she realized there was no real competition here—facts were what she did best—but there was more to winning this case.

What Michael was counting on, which she still needed to earn, was the trust of the good people in Witchland. They had lived in this town for years and had worked hard to be self-sufficient. It was important to them to ensure that the forest was left intact. The towns-folk seemed willing to keep fighting, but they really needed a leader to stand up for them in court and remind those developers that their town wasn't for the taking.

Thankfully, most of the hard work was already done, since Michael had collected dozens and dozens of signatures on a petition along with signed statements from most of the residents of the town opposing the sale of the forest. Hopefully, that petition would give her enough of an edge in court to convince the judge that she had the majority on her side.

Sarah also found that Michael had noticed some odd reports of movement in the forest late at night that he wanted to check out. In a hastily scrawled note on one of the police reports, Michael had wondered if the security camera at the head of the trail had caught something. Sarah made a mental note to ask Officer Eli about that, and her heart fluttered at the thought of talking to the handsome cop again.

All the statements Michael had collected from the town residents were alike in two ways: Everyone seemed to profess complete opposition to the develop-ers' plan and pledge total admiration for the beauty of the forest. The only person who seemed open to the plans was the town mayor, which Sarah found odd.

How could an elected official of Witchland be so unlike the people he led?

One thing she noticed was an unequivocal admiration and trust in Michael's skills. Michael had saved quotes, cards, and notes from people who supported him and wanted to encourage him to do his best in court. Apparently, there had been a town hall meeting regarding the sale of the forest where Michael had vowed to beat the development company in court, and he had been flooded with notes of encouragement afterward.

The townspeople very clearly trusted Michael, and while she wasn't an inexperienced lawyer by any means, it didn't mean they would instantly trust her. She wasn't as good with people as Michael was. She had to have them follow her to court and lend their voices to hers as she fought Michael's battle for him.

Maybe it would be best if I shook some hands and asked for people's statements myself before the next hearing, Sarah thought, standing up as the idea began to make more and more sense in her head. Michael had taught her that people loved to tell their stories; to get them to like you, all you had to do was listen. If she could get the folks here to like her, then they would surely put their trust in her and help her out in court. Besides, if this was to be her new home, she needed to get to know everyone. After all, they all knew who she was.

Turning around before she closed the door, Sarah called out, "Bye, Addie. I'll see ya later after I pick up supplies to make more of your yummy food," as she grabbed the shopping bags that hung on the hook beside the front door.

For the remainder of that day, Sarah moved with complete and total purpose, chasing down most of the people Michael had talked to and even a few he hadn't. With pen in hand and her brain moving just like it used to back in New York, she asked the people why they didn't want a developer taking their land or cutting down their forests. Some of the responses she got were the same as in Michael's notes; others were vastly different than what Michael had written down a few weeks earlier, but all of them showed a passion and a love for the town and the surrounding forest.

As Sarah made her way through the town, she stopped at a tiny house on the edge of town, right on the border of the forest. The house was completely coated in ivy, and its roof appeared crooked. Smoke curled from the chimney, even though it was warm out. An old bird cage teetered on the door, and Sarah started when she realized it contained a crow. The bird cocked its head and surveyed her with a beady eye before croaking and spreading its wings menacingly. She hesitated before lifting her hand to the gargoyle knocker on the door.

The door swung open before she could knock. Before her stood the strange little woman in the pointy hat. Up close, Sarah realized she even had a wart on her nose. How had she grown a wart on her nose? Sarah shrank back as the witch smirked.

"Sarah Spellwood. Nice to see you without those Jimmy shoes!" The woman squinted down at Sarah's feet, then appraised her. "You know what they call a witch at the beach?"

"N—no," Sarah gulped, feeling nervous around this very odd woman.

"A sand-witch!" She began to guffaw.

"Right." Sarah cleared her throat, glancing at the crow, who was now bouncing around his cage.

"Edgar!" the woman rasped, moving forward and practically shoving Sarah out of the way to let the crow out of his cage. "Don't mind him," she said, as Edgar hopped onto her wrist and stepped sideways up to her shoulder.

"What is your name?" Sarah inquired, raising her pen to her notepad.

"They call me Trouble, but I was born as Harriet," she cracked.

"Right. And is that Edgar for—Edgar Allen Poe?"

Sarah peered at the bird, who was now nuzzling Harriet's stringy gray hair.

"You got it! How can I help you today, Miss Lawyer Pants? I see you're up to Michael's old tricks. That man never put down his notepad," Harriet replied, nodding toward the notepad.

"Well"—Sarah began to write down Harriet's name—"I really need to know who might support me in court, and even testify if need be, to the town's love of nature. My intent is to beat John Gonforth in court and block the sale of the forest to—"

"To Tweedledee and Tweedledum?" Harriet guffawed again. "That's what I call those two, Bert and Morris! I threw eggs at them when they came by here, offering me money to resettle." She cackled.

Sarah made a note. "So you would be willing to make an appearance in court?" she pressed.

"Oh, Judge Harcourt has seen too much of me. He declared me a public nuisance after my first stint in jail for disturbing the peace. You know, sometimes that witch's brew is a bit strong, and I was riding my broom around at midnight, whooping and hollering. But it was a full moon! I couldn't very well just stay put!"

"All right, thank you." Sarah forced a smile and a polite nod to Edgar the Crow as she flipped her notepad shut. "Have a good day!" She walked away, shaking her head. *Maybe she has dementia or something,* she thought to herself.

"You don't remember me? Me and your aunt Beth used to play checkers and make witch's brew back in the day!" Harriet hollered after Sarah.

Sarah hesitated, before deciding to push forward, as if she had heard nothing. But looking back, she did have a fuzzy recollection of a very strange lady who used to come over to Aunt Beth's and help her stir frothy teas in a huge cauldron in Aunt Beth's kitchen. They would talk about witchy things, and Sarah would sit under the kitchen table, spellbound by their many references to things she had previously only heard of in movies and shows like *Hocus Pocus*. An even fuzzier memory bubbled to the surface, where she had watched her aunt grumble about leaving the ladle across the room and then float the ladle to her from its resting place on the kitchen table in order to stir the cauldron's contents.

Maybe this stuff is real—no, it can't be! she argued with herself.

"Looks like you tossed the shoes and the lipstick, but that briefcase of yours has city written all over it. You should get a one-of-a-kind woven bag from our local weaver so you don't stand out so much!" Harriet yelled after her.

Sarah waved over her shoulder, eager to put as

much distance between herself and the witchy lady as possible.

Returning to the town square, Sarah felt afraid to knock on doors anymore. Who knew how many other weirdos might bother her? She also felt a bit disconcerted by the memories that kept coming up in her mind.

A woman came running out of the coffee shop with 'Lativia's Javacadabra' painted over its purple door in huge gold letters and ushered for Sarah to come toward her. "Sarah Spellwood! I heard you were taking statements and rallying people for court! How about you come in here and take your statements? I'll call everyone and have them come in to talk to you! Give your feet a rest and have a tea on me."

Sarah smiled graciously and accepted her invitation.

The interior of the coffee shop was sunny and cozy. Sarah was transfixed by the aromas of tea leaves and freshly baked, buttery croissants. An entire wall of tea mixes in jars and huge containers of locally roasted coffee beans sitting behind the counter caught her eye. On the other end of the shop, there was a wall of Salem Witch Trial memorabilia, and on the opposite wall was a collection of black-and-white pictures of the town from the 1930s. The woven wicker furniture looked antique and smelled of fresh lemon wax and lacquer.

"You have such a lovely establishment," Sarah remarked, pausing to survey the pictures of Depression-era Witchland. "There is a lot of history here!"

"Thanks." The woman beamed. "I'm Susie, by the way."

"Nice to meet you, Susie. I don't remember this place being open before?" Sarah said.

"Oh, my partner and I moved here from Vermont and opened this place about five years ago," Susie explained as she moved behind the counter and began to make Sarah a drink. "We tried to play into the witchy theme of this town while also honoring Lativia. So we haven't been here too long, but we sure do love it. Our friends, Margaret and Hua, raved about this place after they moved here, so we thought we'd give it a shot."

"I know Margaret and Hua," Sarah said, smiling as she thought of her quirky but kind neighbors.

"Aren't they just the best? They supply many of our herbs and vegetables," Susie responded. "And our landlady, Daisy, is just the best, too. She owns the apothecary in the back, across the courtyard."

"That name sounds familiar from my childhood summers here." Sarah nodded.

As Sarah meandered to the other wall to look at the series of illustrations from the Salem Witch Trial period, a white cat got up from its bed on the counter and stretched before casually striding toward her over the bakery display case. "Hi, kitty kitty," Sarah cooed, scratching behind the cat's ears as it affectionately ducked into her hand.

"That's Zeva!" the woman declared.

"Hi, Zeva," Sarah said.

Zeva looked at her with intense eyes, and Sarah swore she heard her say hello. She backed away, her heart hammering across her breastbone, terrified that what had happened in the woods was occurring all over again. Susie glanced at her and smiled mysteriously, so Sarah smiled back and struggled to regain her composure.

Sarah followed as Susie led her to a comfortable corner booth with lots of room. Susie set a vegetable sandwich and a steaming hibiscus tea latte in front of her. "Just let me know if you need anything else, dear," Susie chirped.

"Thank you so much," Sarah said, taking in the delightful lunch and trying not to look at Zeva. Zeva was sitting by the cash register with her tail curled around her body, blinking at Sarah playfully. It was hard avoiding her stare.

Susie let Sarah eat and then got on the phone. She made a single call, "Yes, Sarah Spellwood is here. Come on over!" Just as Sarah opened her notepad, countless people began to stream in, crowding around the booth to speak to her.

Man, word sure travels fast here! Susie just called one person and here they all come! Is the whole town here or what? Sarah felt rather amused. She settled back into her booth and listened to all the people talk about their lives and how much the forest had benefited them.

"I was healed by a medical extract that came from a plant in the forest."

"I want to save the habitat for the rare lynx."

"My husband proposed to me on the top of Mount Katribus."

"We have three generations of family living at the edge of the forest in the same house."

"We settled our bean farm long before the white people came."

The stories she collected caused tears to well up in her eyes, which threatened to hit the paper and blur her writing as she struggled to get all the words down.

"Try the magical energy powder! It's better than coffee!" a woman told her with a wink as she concluded her tale of being the daughter of the old sawmill's owner.

She sighed once more and whispered so the woman couldn't hear, "Seriously? 'Magical energy powder' at a coffee shop named after my distant relative? I wonder what else they are brewing here?" Quickly, she squelched her fantasy of a back room filled with a coven of green-faced nutcakes peering into a steaming cauldron and giggled at her own joke. But then Susie brought her a smoothie with the supposed miracle powder, and Sarah's emotional and physical exhaustion at the long day of work instantly cleared. Suddenly, she felt as if she had just woken up and worked out and was ready for a new day. She spent the next several hours conversing with people, attempting to remember all of their names and how they were all related.

When the last of the people had cleared out, Sarah took a few moments to compose herself. It had been an overwhelming and emotional day, but she liked everyone she had met, and she did not feel a bit tired still. One thing was clear: She had to protect this town from becoming an over-developed tourist mecca. The rare lynx living in the forest, the townspeople with history here, the sustainable timber and lumber indus- try, the furniture industry—these things mattered to these people, and losing them would hurt far too many individuals. The revenue that hotels and malls would supposedly bring in would hardly make up for the sentimental value lost, or for the lynx's habitat being gobbled up by bulldozers and cement.

Sarah stood to stretch and walked across the coffee

shop to a glass door in the back that led into a little room. The room was lined with shelves, stuffed with old books. Many of them had words like 'Spells' or 'Witch' in the titles. Sarah stroked the spines of some of the more exquisitely bound books before moving to the glass door that looked out onto the courtyard behind the coffee shop. On the other end of the lovely court-yard, which was full of flourishing flowers, she could see inside a tiny store. Its walls were filled with large mason jars brimming with colorful plant material, and an old-fashioned scale for weighing purchases stood next to an ancient till. Dusty volumes were stacked under the counter. The sign above the door read 'Lativia's Apothecary' in the gilt script of Javacadabra's sign. A large-boned, espresso-skinned woman with dreadlocks, whose bright purple lips matched her huge purple-framed eyeglasses, moved into view; she was behind the counter, mashing something using a mortar and pestle with great concentration. Sarah instantly recognized her as Daisy, one of Aunt Beth's good friends.

I need to go talk to her soon, Sarah thought. *But I don't have time now; I still need to go shopping and make Addie her food.*

Just as she thanked Susie and made her leave to go to the grocery, she noticed an elderly gentleman giving her a friendly, beckoning wave to sit down next to him.

She obliged and opened her notebook once more. *Geez, I hope this is the last interview. I've got to get home and let Addie out,* she thought to herself.

As if on cue, he effortlessly began to share his memories about how he had been taken to the forest as a child to play among the critters that lived there.

"My family is from a long line of craftsmen who came here to use recycled wood to make their goods. Instead of cutting down the trees from the forest, they wanted to allow it to flourish." And with a wink, he whispered, "Sarah, I can even tell you stories about yourself, about your family line. Stories you wouldn't believe. But, my child, that is for later and for you to discover yourself."

Sarah laughed and rolled her eyes playfully. "Well, I'm sure I've heard them all."

"Not all of them," he hinted mysteriously.

Sarah closed her notepad. "Well, I am sure grateful that you all have opened up to me. I have so many testimonies now. Judge Harcourt will surely listen to us now and rule in our favor."

"Well, you *are* Attorney Spellwood after all . . ." he stated. "And you were trained by Michael Howler, so we know we're in good hands." He winked affectionately and squeezed her hand. "Now run along and take care of that mutt," he added jokingly. "Give her a good pet and a hug for me, too. She must sure miss Michael; those two were partners in crime."

"I sure will," Sarah promised.

Sarah walked away feeling happy to know that she was accepted and even embraced as the town's new legal advocate. But she also felt the ever-growing burden of responsibility to so many people. Could she do this?

Like it or not, no court could argue with the emotion and love the townsfolk displayed for the woods around them. Other than a few people, like the mayor whom she wasn't able to sit down with, she had spoken to almost everyone in the town. Well, almost everyone.

Tucking the notebook under her shoulder, Sarah realized that she had to talk to Margaret and Hua still. Surely, they would have a lot to say about all this.

CHAPTER ELEVEN

"THEY'RE STILL GOING THROUGH WITH THIS ridiculous notion of ripping our forest apart. With Michael's passing, rest his soul, I'd at least think they'd table the discussion for a while. Where are these developers, Sarah? I'll show them a thing or two . . ."

"Calm down, Hua," Margaret soothed. "We can't fight this by ourselves, but we can help Sarah. And we'd be better off helping her than tossing eggs at the people threatening our town."

Sarah suppressed her smirk, realizing that Margaret was referring to Harriet.

Hua was steaming with rage as she turned back to the row of plants she was tending inside the greenhouse, shaking her head before pointing to the large tomato vines that took up most of the back corner. "I don't know about eggs, but we've certainly got some ripe tomatoes and could spare a few. Watch me. I will show you some practice shots."

"Hua, we believe you, but let's throw them into a big pot for tomato soup instead of wasting them on the developers," Margaret replied, wiping her sweaty forehead with the back of her gardening glove before turning back to Sarah. "Anyway, Sarah, do you think that you have what you need?"

The two women had been speaking with her for over an hour the morning after her visit to Javacadabra, telling her all about how they had been married at the town hall, had built the greenhouse out of an old barn, and had lived in Witchland for many years now after leaving Manhattan behind. Their love of growing plants, of animals, hiking, and giving back to their community was evident in their opinions and their work.

"Yes, I've got all I need and more." Sarah smiled, her attention momentarily derailed by the colorful flowers in the dirt next to her. "You do have a lovely greenhouse," she commented, tucking her notebook in her briefcase as she began to walk around, admiring the plants that the two women painstakingly tended to.

The greenhouse was more like a botanical garden, with dirt-filled planters crowding together on every table that made up the rows in the room. Labels and pictures showed off what each section was supposed to be, helping to distinguish the plants that often grew up intertwined. The faint smell of manure fertilizer and rich mulch hung in the air, and Sarah could feel the soothing coolness of fine mist on her skin and hair. *So much for my straightening routine this morning! Why do I even bother with my hair anymore? I actually don't even really care about it. I have never felt so free before,* Sarah thought, as she felt her curls begin to frizz.

"We've been running this greenhouse for as long as we've been together." Hua smiled. "It's a nice feeling knowing that we are both responsible for this place. Plus, everyone loves it when we pass around our vegetables or offer up a new recipe we have tried out. We supply all of the restaurants in town, and Geno, a real Sicilian from New York—well, Geno says our tomatoes are the secret to the best marinara he's ever created!"

"It's our own little slice of magical paradise," Margaret added. "Even in the bitter cold and hardships of winter, we try to remember that hope always grows, Sarah. This greenhouse is proof of that."

"That's great advice; I'll keep that in mind," Sarah said, nodding her head.

Sarah wandered through the other sections of the greenhouse. Herbs, flowers, tree saplings . . . they really did have a little of everything, and it all seemed to be growing incredibly well.

Exiting the greenhouse with a fond goodbye to her neighbors, Sarah grinned down at the scads of notes she had taken, and hope sprung to life in her chest. This was why she was working so hard to protect the forest and carry on Michael's legacy, not for fantasy Leekins or talking dogs but because of the people who loved it and depended on it—and on her.

"Addie, I'm home," she called, opening the door to Michael's office and walking two steps before she banged her hip into the side table Michael had placed beside the entrance.

As Addie ran over to greet her, Sarah groaned a little bit and rubbed the bruise forming over her skin. Michael was definitely a lot more durable than she was —this was the third time she had bumped her hip on that table.

"All right, Addie, it's time for a big change," Sarah declared as she placed the golden-mix's food bowl next to her water on the floor.

As much as she loved Michael and wanted to keep his memories intact, this office was hers now, and she might as well start customizing it to her liking.

Placing all the boxes and bins of cases she still had yet to organize in the corner of the room, she began moving furniture around the periphery. The couch went in the corner, the chairs and table from upstairs went by the window, the freezer was moved downstairs and plugged into an outlet on the first floor, and all of Michael's hiking stuff went into a box she would donate later.

Scooting the cabinets around, she opened one and found an old, dusty television that Michael had obviously never used before. He wasn't much for TV, calling the news and talk shows 'glorified nonsense' and claiming the sitcoms and entertainment channels were too extreme for his taste. Clearly he hadn't used this one, judging by the blanket of dust on it. With a mighty heave, she lifted the television up and placed it on a table before finding an outlet and plugging it in.

The old screen switched on, and she let some talking head read her the news for background noise as she continued to move things around to make it comfortable. "Like the new look, Addie?" she asked as she started heating up some minestrone soup from Hua and Margaret and watching bubbles form in the awesome-smelling broth as a wondrous odor wafted through her nostrils. "I'll need to go shopping tomorrow to grab a few more things, but so far the room looks good, right?"

Addie barked at her the second she asked the question, causing her to jump a bit before she noticed a squirrel rushing away from the window.

"That's it. Addie didn't answer me with her bark; she just scared the squirrel away. She couldn't really understand me at all," she mumbled to herself.

Plopping down on the couch with her meal, she smiled. Despite all the work and the progress, and the boatload of more work coming her way, this place felt like home. Her home.

It had been a long time since she had felt like that.

CHAPTER TWELVE

Sarah rolled over in her bed, grimacing at the sound of scraping furniture across the floor. A quick glance at the clock told her it was only three a.m. Placing a pillow over her head, she grumbled in her semi-asleep state as the sounds increased in volume. She finally woke up completely and bolted out of bed when Addie let out a series of short, curt barks.

"What in the name of . . ." she muttered to herself, getting up out of the bed and half sleepwalking down the stairs.

It's probably just the wind scraping against the house or maybe moving one of the porch chairs about, she thought.

She rubbed her blurry eyes to get the sleep out of them before she paused on the bottom step of the stairs to gaze out at the scene before her.

"Oh man, this *can't* be happening!" she cried out loud.

The file cabinets, the desk, the table, and all the chairs were moving on their own across the beautiful oak floor she had painstakingly cleaned the day before.

"Okay, I must be dreaming or sleepwalking. This stuff just doesn't happen in waking life. I am going completely crazy, and if I don't get to the bottom of these shenanigans, I'm going to check *myself* into the looney bin as a nut job. Okay, focus, Sarah. Wake up. This is all a dream."

"Good morning, Sarah!" Addie called, bouncing over to her human with an appeasing look in her eyes. *"I tried to stop them, but they are very determined."*

Sarah stared at Addie for a second. Then her sleepy eyes focused enough in the dark to see that her home was filled with Leekins, and she was indeed awake. The little faeries were moving around the wooden floorboards like overgrown ants, streaming in from under the doors and tramping or flying across the house. They formed columns and managed to heave the furniture around. Sarah realized that they were setting everything back exactly as Michael had had it.

"Oh no, the Leekins are back, and I can hear Addie talking. And I heard that cat talking in the coffee shop earlier! When is this crazy nightmare going to end?"

Sarah hit her forehead with the palm of her hand and hoped this illusion would go away.

Yet, there they were—all up close and way too personal for Sarah's comfort.

Upon closer inspection, some of the Leekins were even wearing acorn tops as hardhats, and it would almost be a comical scene aside from the fact they were undoing a lot of her hard work.

"Clover Figcreek!" Sarah roared, watching the Leekin, who was apparently ordering the workers around from the top of another pyramid.

"Hello, Sarah. We are fixing your mistake." The tiny Leekin smiled, puffing her chest out with a sense of accomplishment.

"What mistake?" Sarah demanded.

"You moved all of Michael's stuff, so we are moving it back."

After hitting her palm to her forehead again, Sarah was now clearly awake. "I moved it for a reason, and you have no right to be in my home moving my stuff," she fumed with her piercing green eyes riveted on Clover Figcreek. "This is my home now, and I want to make it mine, so, please, get out!"

"No! No! No!" The Leekin pouted, stamping her three-toed foot on the back of one of her fellow Leekins. Deciding to ignore the slight yelp of pain from this Leekin, she kept speaking. "This is

Michael's home, not yours. You have to keep it all the same."

"I'm not arguing with you, since you don't exist," Sarah said. *But then, why is the television being carried across the floor by Leekins with a dozen or so pea-sized biceps?* she thought, rubbing her eyes to be sure they weren't deceiving her. "Enough of this nonsense." Her voice cracked with exasperation as she watched the Leekins start to fiddle with the case files she had stacked in the corner. She'd spent far too much of her time organizing that pile to have it undone. "Look, I don't have time for this. Just get out!"

Clover Figcreek shot back, "Don't worry, just wait, and we will fix everything."

"I said get out!" Sarah screamed at the Leekin pyramid, watching it shudder as she began storming toward it. "I'm going to get everything put back myself. GET OUT NOW!" she added, deciding that if her mind was going to keep hallucinating Leekins, she'd at least give them a stern talking to and let them know who the boss was.

"Fine," Clover Figcreek huffed. "But you better put everything back exactly as it was. Or we'll be back." She whistled, leading the Leekin swarm out.

They crawled under the doors and through cracks in the walls, and Sarah mentally reminded herself to seal up the cracks on the off chance this was all real.

Gazing around at her discarded files, boxes, and papers, she began tiredly working to put it all back. Her way.

No tiny creatures were going to talk back to Sarah Spellwood! No one was going to, actually.

This was her home, and she was going to keep it that way.

CHAPTER THIRTEEN

After an early morning of moving furniture, Sarah's brief respite on the couch was interrupted by the ringing phone. Michael still had a landline, so she had to pull herself off the couch and stumble for the phone. Her fingers curled around the receiver as she pulled it to her ear, taking a deep breath as she rubbed her eyes and face.

"Hello?" she asked wearily. Sarah took notice of the fact that she had been sleeping on the couch instead of her bed after the furniture debacle.

Phew, I must be tired.

"Sarah, this is Matthew Lewis, the town mayor. I'm sorry to wake you this early, but the developers have just come by the town hall and are requesting to meet with you sometime before they move forward with their acquisition proceedings. They are curious if you are still continuing Michael Howler's lawsuit to prevent those proceedings. Can you make it down here to meet with them this morning?"

"Sure, sure, I can," Sarah agreed reluctantly, pulling the phone away from her ear to stop a massive yawn from betraying how tired she was, barely hearing the man's goodbye before she hung up. Her head instantly fell into her hands, and she let out a loud groan.

"Great, just great," Sarah grumbled as Addie darted over to her, her eyes filled with curiosity. "I'm tired, haven't eaten, got up at three a.m., and spent half the night reorganizing all my stuff that shouldn't have been moved in the first place. Now I need to prepare to meet with those slimy developers at the worst possible time."

Dodging the piles of Michael's belongings and the furniture she had moved in the night, cursing the Leekins along the way, she grabbed the files she needed and stuffed them into her briefcase. "It's a good thing I know where the files are. At least those annoying and bossy little creatures didn't move them somewhere, never to be found again."

She moved around the house getting everything in order, her movements slightly comatose. She stopped outside the bathroom mirror long enough to brush her teeth, smear some lipstick on, and attempt to calm her hair's explosive curliness before she petted Addie and dashed out the door.

Thankfully, it was still fairly early in the morning, and most people were already in the shops, at work, or hiking the trails. Not too many townspeople were around to see her somewhat disheveled state as she hurried down the streets toward the largest building in the town—Town Hall.

The town hall of Witchland, New Hampshire, was a sight to be seen. Built in 1753 during the late Baroque period, it expressed that period's aesthetic tendency toward extravagance and detail. Massive pillars of ornately carved granite lined its portico, and the building's grounds were ringed by a stellar stone wall built by Italian masons who had migrated to New England earlier in the century. Walking up the steps to the massive oak doors with their polished bronze handles, Sarah had the sensation of walking into a palace. She had always admired this place as a child, and she had loved when her aunt would take her inside just to see the highly polished white marble floors. Sarah had always played a game, trying to follow the veins of black and gray in the white marble with the toes of her shoes.

Sarah swallowed hard as she laid out the plans for her defense in her head. She had thoroughly reviewed Michael's notes, and now she just needed to sound like she hadn't spent less than a few days reading and absorbing the knowledge he had accumulated in order to buy herself and the people of the town a little more time to make their case. "This is just a meet-and-greet, this is just a meet-and-greet, this is just a meet-and-greet," she chanted as if it was part of her morning meditation. *I need to be on my guard, nonetheless. I don't trust John Gonforth, and I am ready if he thinks he can try to twist my words outside of the courtroom. That guy is a Class-A jerk.*

The town hall threatened to swallow her whole as she walked into its massive shadow, turning around to gaze at the town and the surrounding forest. This was what she was fighting for, and this was the cause that Michael had demanded of her. She would just have to rely on her skills and trust that she had enough prowess to present her case clearly and buy herself enough time to prepare an even more thorough defense before appearing in court.

I can do this. I am Sarah Spellwood, for goodness's sake!

As she pushed open the wooden door and walked inside, a woman from behind a large desk glanced up from her computer and smiled at her. "You must be Sarah. Mayor Lewis and the others are waiting for you in the conference room, just down the hall to the left." A perfectly manicured hand reached out to point in the direction before the woman stared at her, attentively waiting for any other questions.

"Thank you." Sarah nodded, noticing herself in a mirror by the desk and smoothing down her clothes and hair before heading down the hallway, her high heels clicking loudly. She followed a large vein in the marble and smiled to herself, a surge of confidence soothing her jitters. She sighted the large conference room on the left and opened the glass door as four men stood up from the wooden table and moved to greet her.

"Ah, Sarah Spellwood, glad to see you made it. Welcome to Witchland, New Hampshire." Mayor Lewis smiled, his thick New England accent already familiar to Sarah from the phone.

He was a short man with graying hair, and although he was dressed in a flannel shirt and jeans, he emitted an aura of being the man everyone listened to. As she shook his hand, he turned toward the other men.

"Gentlemen, Sarah Spellwood will be the one taking over for Michael in the review of your plans for our town's forest. May his soul rest in peace, Michael

Howler was a good lawyer. I know that Sarah is more than capable of filling his shoes."

"That he was. And I've met her." John smiled, inclining his head respectfully at Sarah, seemingly not noticing or caring about the distasteful look Sarah gave him in return. "These are my clients, Mr. Bert Brevil and Mr. Morris Casper of B & M Real Estate. They are prominent developers in the area, and they are the ones spearheading the development of the resort destination."

Sarah was already familiar with these men by name thanks to Michael's detailed case file. Bert and Morris both looked alike—balding, smooth-shaven baby faces, beady brown eyes, tweed business suits, absurd smiles on their faces—as they shook Sarah's hand, treating her just like an old friend. She returned the handshakes, unsure what to think about them—but as Harriet said, they sure did look like Tweedledee and Tweedledum. Yet, they seemed friendly enough—for merciless and greedy developers.

"Hello, Sarah." Bert smiled, squeezing her hand as Morris began to speak, his eyes glinting as he looked Sarah up and down.

"Now, in spite of Michael's unfortunate passing, we would like to move ahead with this incredible deal for the town. By turning over the deeded rights to the 350 acres of town forest, we can create a beautiful business park and residential housing cluster that everyone will benefit from. Just think of the possibilities, Sarah! Tourism is a steady trickle now . . . imagine it turning into a flood! These dingy, impoverished houses will become beautiful mansions, and the town square—imagine this—will turn into a cluster of tourist shops and restaurants! The town will absolutely flourish. You and John could handle all the real estate transactions and have steady and lucrative work for years, even after we've finished building. Heck, you'll be set for life just with the work we have for you alone! Our cash offer still stands, of course. One million dollars going into the town coffers straight away, not to mention the hundreds of thousands of dollars from tax revenue that will come in every year. Just sign this Concession of Declaratory Interest form right here and everything will be complete," he said with a proud smile, shoving a contract and a pen toward her as he pointed at where she would have to sign. It was obvious he thought he had presented the perfect pitch, one Sarah would be insane to turn down.

"Wait a moment, Mr. Casper," Sarah interrupted, slowly pushing the form back across the table. "Michael might be dead, but that doesn't mean I'm just going to stand aside and be railroaded into agreeing to concede to your terms. Your proposed plan would destroy acres upon acres of pristine forest, eliminate the homes of hundreds of animal species, terminate the town's primary source of income, which is timber for the mill, and pollute the waters of Witch's Brook from stormwater runoff, which will affect neighboring towns in ways we can't even imagine right now. It could also have huge negative health effects for both the people and wildlife in the area.

"People depend on trees in this forest as the source of high-quality, old-growth timber that they carefully turn into fine handmade furniture. They've been tending this forest for over two centuries for this purpose, and you want to turn it into a parking lot? I have statements and a petition from almost every citizen of Witchland. All of them expressed an extreme dislike and disapproval for your proposed plan. Would you like to look over them yourself, or shall I read them aloud?" She smiled at her opponents, who were frantically shaking their heads as they glanced at the papers before she continued. "This town thrives on the wood products industry, and your plan would severely disrupt that. You say your development in the long term will make the town tons of money, but in the short term, all I can see are losses.

"Unless you relocate your project and scale it down, I will be asking the judge to issue an order for you to complete a comprehensive environmental impact statement. And I promise you, once you present that report and the testimonies that I have collected from townspeople, the judge will block this deal. You and I both know that townspeople have confirmed sightings of Canada Lynx in the area, an animal the judge well knows is on the endangered species list. How do you plan to get away with developing its prime habitat when it comes time to obtain proper federal permits?"

As she spoke, she pulled out the various notes and documents that supported her claim as well as her statements from town residents about lynx sightings, laying them out one by one in front of the developers. Their frowns deepened with each piece of paper she produced.

Morris smiled at her, although his grin was noticeably cynical. The corners of his lips didn't even curl toward his eyes as his voice became slippery and condescending. "Well, Sarah. You've certainly done your homework, but you overlooked one small detail. Shall I remind you what lies in the town's very own charter?" he said, looking directly into the eyes of the mayor. "Ordered and timely development shall be allowed by permit and decree for the public health and welfare of its citizens." Morris sneered with a slow and careful emphasis on the word 'welfare.' "Welfare? Heck, we're talking economics here, Sarah. The money flowing into this town from the hotel room bookings alone will provide triple what the town makes from making furniture in half the time."

Sarah noticed the spit flying from between his yellowed teeth and landing on her papers. She had to breathe hard not to gag.

"With an established big-name hotel as the anchor," Bert added, "more and more people will be able to stay here and spend money, and the local shops and businesses will thrive."

Morris added, "The furniture factory barely makes enough to support the town. Just think of all the cheaper goods the rest of the stores could sell if more people came to the area. You guys would even get a Walmart!" Morris grabbed his handkerchief out of his pants pocket and wiped the back of his neck. "Shop-keepers will flourish, the town will become a destina-tion resort, and the value of real estate will soar. This is what this project will bring to the town."

Money, money, money, Sarah hissed to herself, listening to the two men prattle on and on as they showed her projected yield statistics and cost-benefit flowcharts. Granted, it was a lot of cash that would boost the town, but they were missing the point. Money could be made almost anywhere, but a beau-tiful forest filled with old-growth trees and endangered animals, or a handmade wooden chair . . . those were unique and special.

The people of the town, its current raft of visitors, and people like her understood the value of the town setting and the fact that this remarkable way of life couldn't be found anywhere else. No amount of money was worth compromising their pristine views, their long walks on lazy days, or the peaceful lifestyle each of them lived.

"Witchland would morph from a unique and magical place into something foreign, something like every other town that transformed itself into a commercialized getaway vacation spot. It would lose its charm, and that is too high a price to pay," Sarah pointed out.

As the developers—who continued to remind Sarah of Tweedle-dee and Tweedle-dum—quieted down, she cracked a gradual smile as she stared into their eyes with her signature look that quickened their silence. From her briefcase, she pulled a well-worn file which had Michael's scrawl all over it. She flipped it open, and the three men across from her waited with impatience for her to speak again.

"I understand that you have hired a well-known big-game hunter to work for you: a Mr. Dismas Lorian," she continued. "He is apparently a wildlife consultant for your development company, correct? Wouldn't it be ironic if the wildlife report you have to file with the government reveals that there are no lynx in the forest—a report that is written by a famous hunter and trapper of large cats?"

"What exactly are you implying, Ms. Spellwood?" John seethed.

"There aren't any lynx in these woods." The deep and gravelly voice that spoke up behind Sarah instantly caused shivers to run down her spine. She swiveled in her chair to find herself face to face with a tall, muscular man clad in khaki pants, black laced boots, and a camo shirt. Her head only reached his stomach as she slowly raised it, taking in the massive hunter. If his size wasn't intimidating enough, he was also sporting a long hunting knife strapped to his belt in a black sheath. His hands looked like massive bear paws as he cracked his knuckles and stared down at Sarah through reflective, aviator sunglasses that concealed his eyes, but Sarah could tell from his expression that his eyes blazed with aggression and contempt.

Sarah visibly gulped, not only because he was staring down at her with a look that could kill, but because, oddly enough, she almost found him intriguing. Not attractive, mind you, but intriguing in a 'wow, this is one huge man' kind of way. An "eh hem" from the mayor brought her back to her senses as she realized she was staring up at this man with her mouth agape.

"W—well, uh, er . . ." Sarah stumbled, clearing her

throat abruptly before taking a deep breath and regaining her composure quickly. "That's a bold threat on a species that is endangered. Michael has a file detailing your work with B & M Real Estate. It states that you are a wildlife consultant hired by the very company that wants to develop the land. And I also see you often visit the hunting lodge and hunt on the four hundred acres next to Mount Katribus that sits adjacent to the Witchland Forest. Wouldn't this be seen as a conflict of interest?" she said confidently, feeling back in her game.

"You got proof of that, Ms. Spellwood?" Dismas growled, gazing down at her as Sarah began to leaf through the file on her lap, which somehow lacked the document she needed. She cursed under her breath, but loud enough to elicit a few snickers from Bert and Morris.

"I must have left it at home," Sarah muttered, embarrassment falling over her face like a red cloud as she sighed heavily.

"Why don't you go and get it?" suggested the mayor helpfully over the objections of the other gentlemen.

"But, Mr. Mayor, she is totally unprepared," John Gonforth objected loudly as he sat back and smirked.

"She is new to this town and the case," the mayor reasoned. "She has only been here for a few days, and I want to give her a chance to get organized. If we're going to court over this, I want to have all the facts in front of me first. Then we can decide what to do with the information."

Sarah nodded in thanks and began to speed-walk out of the room, her mind already spinning as she ran from the town hall. Those partnership and land ownership papers were as clear as day in her head, but why weren't they in the folder? She knew she'd seen them before. But where had she put them?

CHAPTER FOURTEEN

ADDIE HOPPED UP FROM HER NAP AS SARAH rushed through the door. Sarah was muttering to herself about the consultancy agreement as she began to tear through the organized piles she had created, flipping through folders and throwing papers to the ground. "Where are those files?" she screamed. "If those little Leekins were messing around with my stuff again I am going t—t—to—Addie, what is it?"

Sarah's panic caused Addie to whine and droop her tail a bit. If the Leekins were here, they could help her talk to Addie and tell her where those papers were and if she was wasting her time looking in the wrong place. Sarah then realized with a slight panic that she had begun to think of the Leekins and Addie's talking as real, not hallucinations or figments of her imagination.

Just as Sarah thought that, Addie lowered her nose to the ground, ran right over to a file, and made exaggerated snout noises to get Sarah's attention.

Addie barked out loud, looked at Sarah, and then looked down. "Did you find something, Addie?" asked Sarah as Addie ran over to her, wagged her tail, and then ran back to put her paw right on top of the file.

"Well, look at that," exclaimed Sarah as she opened up the folder.

She remembered that she had put those papers in the 'Lynx' file for safekeeping, and luckily, the Leekins hadn't gone about moving them yet. "I must be more forgiving to those Leekins, even if they are pesky little figments of my imagination," she muttered.

As Addie exhaled in frustration about Sarah's comments, a familiar buzzing filled Sarah's ears. The buzzing meant the Leekins were nearby. "Well, I guess I am going to have my chance again. If they come close enough, then maybe they could help me talk to Addie."

She saw Addie lift her nose to sniff at the Leekins' unique, earthy scents, and out of the corner of her eye, she spotted several of them poking about on the upstairs windowsill.

"Addie?" Sarah tentatively tried, but she received no audible response.

Addie lay still, sniffing toward the stair. The Leekins were probably too far away for their magic to allow Addie to talk, but Sarah didn't have time to wait for them to come down from that sill.

Sarah ran up to the windowsill, bent over so she could see which Leekin was running around, and secretly hoped it would be the most irritating and bossy of them all.

Clover Figcreek stepped out upon the windowsill, stared up at Sarah, and started complaining right away. "I have been watching you make a mess of Michael's perfectly organized papers by dumping them on the floor. Although Addie vouched for you the last time we were here, I still need some convincing that Michael made the right choice for you to be his successor and guard the forest and town of Witchland. Now I'm not so sure. Sarah, you are making such a mess."

"What makes her think she could just come in and move stuff around?" Addie heard Clover Figcreek whisper to another Leekin. "Do you think she's got what it takes to keep us safe?"

Addie barked, causing Sarah and the Leekins to look up. This time, Sarah could hear Addie as clearly as the Leekins: *Enough, you guys. Let's get that file to Town Hall. We've got more important business to attend to right now. Let's save the forest, instead of worrying about messes!*

The file Sarah needed was right on the floor where Addie had found it. She bent down, lifted it up carefully, checked that a copy of the Dismis's deed and consultancy agreement was in there, and dashed off.

As Sarah sprinted up the steps to Town Hall and opened the big wooden door, she took a breath and walked inside, trying to calm herself down before going into the conference room. It was essential that she not appear flustered.

Reentering the conference room, she laid the open folder down and pointed to the wildlife assessment contract that Michael had copied with Dismas Lorian's name right below Bert's and Morris's. "There's your proof, Mr. Lorian."

"That means nothing," John bellowed, wringing his hands helplessly as he stared at the mayor. "Mayor, please. This proves nothing," he pleaded. "Mr. Lorian completed that wildlife study for us over a year ago, well before he knew what we were going to do. The report he filed is legitimate. There are no lynxes out there, and we've got solid evidence to prove that is the case."

Sarah opened her mouth, about to deliver a scathing retort, before the door opened and the mayor's aide poked her head in, motioning to Mayor Lewis.

"Excuse me, Mr. Mayor, but the police chief is calling, and he says it's urgent."

As the mayor walked out of the room, Sarah took a breath, trying to remain calm as John gave her a haughty look. "You know you can't win," he added, his tone dripping with arrogance and authority. "You don't have a legal leg to stand on, whereas I've got state permits and approvals on my side, not to mention the unlimited capacity of one of the largest development companies in the state. What chance do you have?"

"Unlike you, John, I'm not doing this to grease my pockets. I'm doing this to honor the hard work and memory of Michael Howler and to finish something in the best interests of all the townsfolk who have confided their trust in me," Sarah shot back, eyes flashing, while watching him squirm slightly under the glare of her green eyes.

The door opened again as Mayor Lewis stepped back inside. "That was our police chief, and he wants Sarah to come down to the station right away. I'm tabling this discussion until the day after tomorrow."

"You can't do that!" Dismas yelled, his muscles rippling under his shirt in anger. "Not when the land deal is so close to being made."

"What the police chief found could have ramifications on the case, and I believe it bears investigating," the mayor conceded. "Now, I will see you all later once the investigation is complete."

Sarah watched her four opponents walk out of the room and heard them mutter to themselves before she followed them out and headed down to the police station. "We will be seeing you soon," Morris told her sneeringly before they walked off toward their bed-and-breakfast.

Taking a deep breath of relief, Sarah reassured herself, *Thanks for this small miracle. Now I have more time to prepare a proper defense, deal with the missing lynx, and maybe even have some time to deal with all these fantastic hallucinations I seem to be having. Right now, we need all the help and evidence we can get.*

CHAPTER FIFTEEN

The police station was a small building with a professional look to it, fitting nicely with the rest of the town's architecture. Large iron letters spelled out the words 'Police Station' over the entrance. Sarah quickly opened the metal door and walked inside. Aware she was going to twist her left earring in anticipation of seeing Eli again . . . she quickly stopped the urge.

Twin desks were the first thing she noticed when she entered, sitting underneath a bulletin board announcing the events in town. The room was painted blue and white, and the sounds of fingers tapping on a keyboard cut through the air. She stepped toward the desk where a brunette woman in uniform sat, unsure what to do or say. There was no sign of Eli.

The brunette looked up from her computer, and with a smile, stood up.

"Are you Sarah?" she asked, awaiting her nod. "If you'd follow me. I'm Jenna, deputy of Witchland's local law enforcement."

With this brief introduction complete, Jenna led her into the back room where Eli was standing over a bunch of photos. After a moment, the faint sound of typing resumed.

The police chief was deeply engrossed in something on his desk, and as Sarah peered over Eli's muscular shoulder, her hand flew to her mouth as she saw pictures of Michael's body. There, as clear as could be, was an image of him sprawled out at the bottom of the staircase in his home.

"Hello, Sarah." Eli smiled sadly, the concerned gaze he gave her smoothing over the negative thoughts that had just entered her brain. "Sorry I had to call you in like this, but the coroner just finished Michael's autopsy, and I thought it might bring you some comfort to know we confirmed how he died. He sustained a serious blow to the back of his head. How that blow happened is still unclear. We think perhaps he hit his head on the stairs as he fell down."

Letting out a long exhale, Sarah looked at the pictures with teary eyes as she digested the information.

"He didn't suffer much, and he was getting over an ankle injury that made him unsteady on his feet, so that seems to be a perfectly logical explanation," Eli said. "A sad tragedy, but also an understandable one."

Sarah couldn't shake the feeling that was growing in the pit of her stomach. A feeling that was all too familiar, that warned her she needed to look more closely at the facts and trust her intuition.

As she took the autopsy report from Eli to read over it herself, her forehead creased in confusion. "Eli," she stammered, cursing the catch in her voice as she tried to form coherent sentences around the man. "It says he hit the back of his head, but your photos show him lying on his front."

Eli nodded, and Sarah saw confirmation of her suspicions in the wrinkle on his brow. "Well, we figure he may have hit the back of his head when he tumbled down the stairs, before landing on his front."

"But surely a blow that could kill him would leave blood, especially since he fell on a hard surface like the stairs. His skin doesn't even show any internal bleeding that would normally occur from such an event." Sarah forced herself to look harder at the photo that showed the severe bruising on the back of Michael's head. "Your photos don't show any blood on the stairs above him, or any signs that he tried to catch himself as he fell." Sarah walked along the collection of photos, peering at each one. "Plus, if he had fallen backward at the bottom and hit his head, he would have stayed still, or at least not have turned over on his front."

"There is something else about this that I find odd," Eli went on, turning to stare deeply into her eyes, and for a moment she blushed and forgot what she was about to say. The words simply dried up in her mouth as she gazed at the handsome man who seemed to be hanging on to her every word. "The blow to the back of his head was sustained from a medium-velocity blow. That would be hard to get from whacking your head on stairs. Possible, but not easy. Michael would have had to have done something like a gymnastics flip down the stairs."

"I really think that Michael's death might be a bit more than a slip-and-fall," Sarah responded, feeling chills running through her entire body. "What if he was bludgeoned and then fell down?"

Eli was surveying her intensely. "There is another reason I called you down here, actually, and that's because I want to know if Michael had any enemies."

"I'm not saying he had actual enemies, but . . . John Gonforth was his fierce rival. I find it odd that one day, Michael's dead, and the next, Bert and Morris are using Michael's death as a free pass to push their resort agenda," Sarah queried. "Are all land developers that heartless? Or do they know something we don't? And remember the note I gave you?"

"I understand your suspicion," Eli replied seriously, laying a hand on her shoulder. "And I know you're defending the town. We have to be sure about this before we go around making wild claims—even with the note you found. We've got to find hard evidence of wrongdoing if we're going to move ahead with a murder theory. You understand that, don't you?"

"Of course, I do, Eli. I am an attorney," Sarah said, looking away and feeling patronized as she tried and failed to fight back a blush. Eli's hand fell away from her shoulder.

As he led her out to the front of the police station, Eli assured her he was going to look more into this and give Michael's death the attention it deserved.

Sarah smiled. "Thank you, Eli. I just want to know all the facts about Michael's death."

As she left the station, she failed to notice the pair of eyes following her as she began to walk back to her home.

CHAPTER SIXTEEN

Sarah opened the door to her home and slumped against the door, her hand reaching down to pet Addie. "I know Michael was murdered. There is truth to that note you found in New York," she whispered, hearing Addie's low whine.

Sarah's head began to swim. Eli was now suspicious, too. Understanding that Michael might have been murdered was neither helping her put his death behind her, nor helping her sleep at night. Why did her amazing mentor have to meet such an unfair and cruel end?

"Maybe I'm just working too hard and letting the improbable overtake my view of reality. It could have been just a tragic accident and that was all. Michael wasn't murdered, Addie can't talk, and the Leekins were simply my brain's way of coping with being lost in the forest. My brain seems to be doing a lot of coping nowadays, so maybe I'm just overly tired," Sarah reminded herself.

"You can't talk or understand me," she muttered to Addie, trying to forget the scene from earlier where the Leekins had been manipulating and moving all her belongings. She was sleep deprived, and that didn't help. Besides, she'd expended a lot of energy at the crack of dawn to move everything back the way she had placed it. She was also exhausted from the meeting with the lawyers as well as her meeting with Eli.

Sleeping for a good long while would hopefully help her deal with all this. It was ten o'clock, just late enough to justify her going to bed 'early.' She flicked on the television and let the sound of a cooking show fill the house, just to give her some background noise to keep her company.

She hugged Addie, letting the dog lick her face before she frowned, gazing up the stairs with a sense of dread. Tragic accident or not, Michael had still died on that staircase. How was she supposed to climb them now, knowing what she knew, feeling the tingling that she felt? Nothing of importance was really up there, and she could easily turn the two-story building into a one-story building and simply forget the upstairs area existed.

Her eyes turned toward the couch, her palm

pressing into the lumpy cushion as she felt the spongy material. It was comfortable, but she did need a pillow and blanket from her bed to truly get the sleep she deserved. That meant going upstairs.

A shudder passed through her, and her palms began to sweat as she gazed at the steps and into the darkened upstairs. "This is stupid. I'm from Manhattan, for gosh sakes. I conquered my fear of the dark years ago working late nights in the law firm," Sarah said to herself, her shaky limbs pushing her body up as she walked toward the staircase.

She just needed to get upstairs, grab her pillow and blanket, and come back down. She'd done it countless times before. Why did one little fact about Michael's death make so much of a difference in how she lived in her own home?

She walked up the stairs on shaky legs while Addie looked on in concern. Near the top, she suddenly lost her balance, and her hands shot out to grab the railing. That was close. Sarah now moved slower and with purpose, taking each of the last steps as if she was climbing a mountain. It wasn't until her feet touched the floor of the upstairs bedroom that she finally allowed herself to take a deep breath.

She snatched her pillow and blanket from the bed and then noticed the vial. It was still there, still filled with mysterious swirling liquid. This was not a dream, or a hallucination. This was all real. She decided to grab the vial as well as her book from the nightstand and then began to slowly shuffle back down the stairs. Her back was pressed against the wall, almost as if she herself was a part of it, as she half walked and half slid down to the bottom floor, trying to ignore the images in her brain of Michael tumbling down the same stairs. She wasn't Michael, and as long as she had sure footing, she would not share his fate.

"There is no one else in the house with me, and I am perfectly safe," she reminded herself. Stepping down onto the floor with an exhale, Sarah looked down at Addie, who stared up at her with a confused expression.

"I'm going to sleep on the couch, Addie," she added, unsure why she felt the need to explain herself to her dog as she made up her bed on the sofa. "I'm going to sleep right here, safe and sound, until Michael's death is solved. I know he didn't fall on his own, Addie, and I bet you know who killed him. Once I figure this out, I will find the courage to climb those stairs again."

After her bed was made, she padded over to the fridge in the real kitchen. *I can't believe Michael actually set up a makeshift kitchen in his upstairs bathroom. He sure liked his food to keep it that close!* She giggled to herself, remembering his fondness for takeout in

New York when they would work late into the night, reviewing old cases together.

Opening the refrigerator door, she couldn't wait to taste the dinner she had bought at the farmer's market the previous day. Humming to get rid of her growing sense of unease, Sarah savored every bite of the dinner she reheated on the yellow vintage gas range she remembered Michael had been so in love with. She remembered him calling her the moment he found it at an antique shop in Greenwich Village when he visited her five years prior in the city. It was cute and in perfect condition. "It feels really special to be cooking on this stove that Michael so loved, Addie. But it doesn't look like he used it much."

After a delicious dinner, Sarah laid back on the sofa with a book in her hands, her mind in a thousand different places as she felt Addie curl up at her feet. Normally, reading mystery novels helped calm her mind down, especially after a long day in the courtroom. But now that her life was embroiled in one big mystery of its own, it wasn't the same.

She reflected on her current predicament. These types of troubles—murder mysteries, magic, and talking beasts—they all belonged in books, not plaguing normal people like her. She'd moved away from the city not only because of Michael's last request, but also to simplify and get away from life's problems. Yet, now that she had, it didn't seem like life was letting her escape trouble or the big city so easily. She glanced at the vial, wondering what the heck was in it.

Once she finished a chapter, Sarah closed the book with a heavy sigh and reclined on the couch. One arm pulled the covers over her shoulders as her second arm put the book on the floor beside her. As she turned over, she grabbed the vial and gave it a good hard look.

"If the Leekins are just a figment of my imagination, how did this vial end up in my pocket?" she said to a sleeping dog.

The liquid swirled in the glass as she moved it around, nice and thick like maple syrup. Her fingers gripped the vial, and she uncorked it with a pop. It smelled quite earthy, but other than that, it seemed to have no other obvious properties. It was golden and didn't look like any water or drink Sarah had ever seen before. Maybe it was a type of perfume or something.

As she held the vial up to her eyes, a certain thirst sprang into her throat, a thirst she could not ignore. Somehow she knew that the liquid in the vial was bringing this on and that it was safe to drink.

As Sarah sniffed the vial again and inhaled its earthy scent, she glanced down at Addie, who was now looking at her intently. Even if she wanted to ask her dog about whether she should go ahead and drink the liquid in the vial, she couldn't. Surprisingly, the look in Addie's eyes seemed to be encouraging her to go ahead.

Sarah took a deep breath and slowly tipped the contents of the vial into her mouth. The liquid was smooth and silky, and slowly, it slid down onto her tongue as she swallowed. As soon as the sweet taste touched her throat, it lit a fire inside her stomach. The taste was unlike anything she had ever had before, unlike any fruit, candy, or spice she'd ever tasted. Thoughts of cinnamon and vanilla came to mind, but she brushed those away fairly quickly, as the taste certainly was a thing of its own.

She finished swallowing the last drop and placed the vial on the end table. Whatever it was, it tasted good and didn't seem to produce any ill effects. At least, not right away. Yawning as a fresh wave of exhaustion washed over her, Sarah snuggled into her blankets and let the inner warmth spread deep inside her stomach. The warmth seemed to soothe her muscles and burn away her fears.

Sarah wasn't sure how long she slept, but it was a deep and restful sleep. The glow in her stomach pulsed lightly with her breath, and for the first time in a long while, she felt at complete and utter peace.

Smash! Crack! Crash!

Addie and Sarah were abruptly awakened by the sound of shattering glass. It immediately wiped out any remnants of the cozy inner fire created by the Leekins' elixir from the night before.

Sarah struggled to shake herself awake and stand up. This was quite a challenge, given the deep sleep which had overtaken her.

Addie was alert, though—ears perked, eyes staring toward the back door. With hackles raised, she let out a low, menacing growl.

"A—Addie?" Sarah barely breathed out of fear of being heard. "I hear footsteps inside the h—h—house . . ." Then, as if on cue, the sound of slow footsteps in the back room stopped.

Sarah tossed the blanket off as she half ran, half

stumbled across the heaps of files and papers, heading for Michael's cane he always kept on a hook by the front door. The cane was the only thing that she could think of that would work as a weapon, and now she was glad she remembered where it was. Seizing the gnarled piece of wood silently, she held it like a bat as she inched toward the back door.

Walking down the hall toward the back door, Addie's growls led her slowly forward as Sarah's brain snapped fully awake with adrenalin. *You would expect something like this to happen in New York,* she thought to herself, *yet it never did. So why now in this not-so-sleepy little town?*

Addie growled, and the front door burst open behind Sarah with the sound of breaking wood, the lock snapping off as a man rushed inside. His features were obscured by darkness, but there was no mistaking his hostile intent as he charged toward her.

With a shriek, Sarah brought the cane down on the man's head. Her strength was born of complete desperation. He grunted in pain and took an unsteady step back, clearly stunned. Sarah backed away, only to be attacked from behind by a second intruder who came from the back door where she heard the glass shatter.

Instantly, the right hand of the second man clamped down on her wrist, forcing her to drop the cane as his left hand reached around and covered her face with a wet rag. Although she'd never succumbed to it before, she instantly knew the smell of chloroform as the sweet odor overwhelmed her senses and made her head swim dizzily. Her legs began to buckle beneath her when, suddenly, the rag dropped away, and her attacker yelled in pain. Addie had clamped her jaws around his leg. Sarah charged forward, sheer desperation allowing her to knock the second intruder aside as she rushed out of the house, barely missing the clumsy grasp of the first intruder.

The fresh air slowly cleared her head as she sluggishly attempted to run down the garden path in front of her house. Surely someone like Margaret or Hua had heard all the noise and was coming to investigate. But before Sarah could open her mouth to scream for help, she tripped over her wobbly feet and landed facedown on the brick path. The man from inside stepped over her back, and this time, his massive, strong arms held her still. Since she couldn't put up much of a fight, her arms and legs flailed for a brief moment as her eyes closed against her will. The last thing she heard was a deep, gravelly voice state:

"Got that pooch with a tranquilizer dart from my gun. It won't be making too much noise for a couple hours at least."

Another familiar voice answered him, "Good. By this time tomorrow, all our problems will be solved."

When Sarah's eyes opened, she noticed two things about her surroundings.

The first was that she was bound to a slippery fake-leather chair, like a doctor's office waiting room chair, with rope around her hands and feet. Her mouth was taped shut with duct tape.

The second was a medical diploma on the wall in a gilt frame. Underneath the diploma was a counter with jars of large Q-tips and tongue depressors.

Sarah wanted to try to struggle and break free, but her limbs refused to move. The entire room seemed to be on its side as she raised and shook her head, wincing at the pain this simple movement caused.

"Ah, you're awake, Sarah. Good," grunted a nearby man in a low voice.

As Sarah struggled to lift her head, she felt rough, cold hands grab her around the throat. The thick fingers were male, and they moved up to her chin and forced her head up. There, before her, stood John Gonforth. His sleazy smile filled her limited vision, and she snarled, her head still throbbing, as John chuckled.

Yet, he wasn't alone. Who was holding up her head?

"If you had only agreed to work with us, or at least

to stand down, none of this would have happened," John chided. He nodded to the man holding her head up, and he let go, allowing her head to flop back down. "But now you'll simply have to have a little accident and share your mentor's fate. It was really a shame he had to die. He was a worthy rival in this otherwise boring, little, pathetic town."

"Why are you doing this?" Sarah forced out. She was painfully aware of how slurred and weird her words sounded.

"Why?" John laughed. "Because we want this development to succeed. And do you know why we want this development to succeed, Sarah? Because there's nothing happening here. Nothing. All the work here involves a few house sales every year, and the occasional estate sale. But, of course, everyone went to Michael for those deals because he was so nice and such a team player." John's sarcasm was scathing. "These country hicks don't understand how the law really works. It's cunning, ruthless, and cold. You have to win at all costs.

"When outsiders come to this town, they bring their land problems with them. Land problems equal cases, which equals a chance for me to take those cases, rise up out of this crummy town, and then become the richest real estate lawyer in the state." He squatted down to Sarah's level. "If I have to cut down a hundred forests and leave animals without their home to get what I want, then that is what I will do."

Stepping back rather gracelessly, he moved past her to rummage around in the drawers behind her. He pulled out a needle and syringe as Dismas walked over to help. With a hammer, Dismas broke the lock on a cabinet full of medicine vials and bottles.

"This happens all the time." John smiled. "A drug addict moves to a new town, fresh start. Gets clean, fools everyone, and then relapses. After your tolerance went down, you just couldn't handle the dose of morphine you injected straight into your arm."

As Sarah weakly struggled against the bonds, trying to force her sluggish muscles to move, John directed Dismas, "Get the disinfectant, too. I'll fix your leg bite and then we'll lay low until she's found. Be sure to fill that bottle with a little more morphine after you're done and plant it beside her. I'll meet you back at the law firm."

"Okay," Dismas muttered, handing the disinfectant to John and accepting the syringe full of morphine from him.

John cast a cruel smile at Sarah before leaving.

Dismas grabbed her arm with his monstrous hand. There was no fighting against him, especially with the chloroform still in her system. "Stay still, Sarah. I promise this will only hurt for a second."

Sarah groaned and moaned as the needle descended down toward her arm. Her eyes closed as her struggles became weaker until, finally, the needle pressed into her skin.

Snap!

Sarah opened her eyes as the needle completely snapped off the syringe, flying away toward the wall as Dismas looked at the morphine harmlessly dripping onto the floor.

"What the hell?" he cursed, storming over to the cabinet to grab a new syringe and fill it with more morphine. "I knew I should have just shot you!"

Looking down, Sarah stared at her arm, noticing that it looked different. Even with her blurry vision and slight dizziness, it looked like the bark of a tree. The texture was rough and coarse, and it was obviously hard, but but when she touched her arm it felt no different from her actual skin. What was odder still was how the texture was spreading across her skin from her neck to her toes. As she raised her head, she resisted the urge to scream in shock from this apparent hallucination.

It wasn't painful or restricting in the slightest, and if she hadn't looked down at her arm, she wouldn't have even known it was happening. Her brain scrambled for facts, for some insane reason as to why this was all happening, and found none until the words of the Leekins flashed in her head.

We shall give you the same gift we gave Michael!

The potion from the Leekins was turning her skin into bark—which meant they were real. It also meant their magic was real, and the forest where they and the lynx lived was being threatened by murderers posing as developers.

The Leekins had given her the power of their forest, and somehow it was turning her skin into the bark of a tree. The Leekins and everything she had dreamed of or imagined—it had all actually happened.

A strange thought filled Sarah's mind as she turned to stare at a potted plant on the windowsill. She saw the flower in the pot lean toward her as if it was leaning toward the sun. It seemed unnatural, but she heard it say inside her mind that it was awaiting her order. Immediately, an order formed in her brain, and almost painfully, she decided to indulge it.

Plant, stop Dismas Lorian! she thought, just as Dismas turned back toward her with another full syringe.

The potted plant obediently launched itself forward like a missile, slamming into Dismas's head, shattering into pieces, and causing the towering man to hit the ground—out cold. Sarah began to flex her arms, feeling the effects of the chloroform disappear completely as she snapped the ropes off. New strength she had never felt before quickly pulsed through her veins. Strength she thought just might be enough to get out of this predicament alive to defend Witchland.

She stood up, felt powerful and resilient, and . . . and . . .

Sarah staggered a bit when the bark-like texture to her skin quickly faded. She took a deep breath, weary despite the new strength which she could still feel. Rubbing herself down to check for any more injuries and finding none, tears filled her eyes at the fact that she was still alive. Miraculously, she had evaded John's attempt to murder her. If he and his developer mates tried to kill her, they had most likely killed before.

She began to shake with adrenalin and residual horror at what had just transpired. This new feeling made her swoon slightly as she sat back down in the chair. She had almost been killed, Michael had been murdered, the potion the Leekins had given her was magical, and Addie could talk. This night was living proof of the fact that magic existed in this town and that Witchland was well worth saving.

"Addie!" she suddenly cried out loudly, running out of the doctor's office just as the sun was starting to rise. Her thoughts were riveted to her dog. If they had harmed her in any way, then they'd have one unbelievably angry woman—no, they'd have one unbelievably angry *witch* with scary new strength and the ability to turn to bark when threatened—to contend with.

Oddly enough, the rising sun seemed to make her run faster. She reached her home in just a few minutes. When she skidded to a halt in front of her door, she didn't even feel out of breath, like she hadn't run at all.

Despite the early hour and the panic churning in her gut from almost dying a few minutes before, her heart rate still rose to high alert when she thought about her dog. For now, urgency was the only emotion she felt. In the back of her mind, she knew she should be feeling tired beyond belief, but maybe the adrenaline hadn't worn off yet. Or maybe this night, and the potion in the vial, had changed her forever.

Moving quickly up the steps toward her home, she pushed open the broken door to find Jenna and Eli standing in the living room, with the town doctor and the local veterinarian kneeling over Addie's motionless form.

"Sarah!" Eli shouted in relief, and for a moment, Sarah became a little light-headed. *Was Eli worried about me?* she wondered, while twisting her left earring out of habit. "I really have to stop twisting my earring."

"What?" asked Eli perplexed.

"Oh, nothing," replied Sarah, making a promise to herself she would stop her sophomoric habit when in the presence of Eli.

"Anyhow, your neighbors called in what they thought might have been a scuffle at your house, so we came over to investigate. What happened here?" questioned Eli.

"John Gonforth and Dismas Lorian," she spat out, "they abducted me. Addie bit one of them—" She broke off, leaning down to make sure her dog was all right as the doctor pulled himself away.

Addie looked up at Sarah with half-drugged eyes, her tail wagging feebly as her tongue slipped out to lick Sarah's hand. Sarah breathed a huge sigh of relief. She wove her fingers through her dog's fur, then she nestled down and gave Addie a big hug. "Thank my lucky stars, you are okay."

"Addie's fine," the vet said, "but she seemed to be hit with some kind of powerful tranquilizer. Apparently, your attackers took the dart with them. She just needs a few minutes to shake it all off, and she'll be all right for the time being."

"We can go to my office," said the town doctor. "It's

closer than the vet's office, and I have some supplies in my office that should patch all this up."

"That's a good idea," the vet added.

"The office," Sarah echoed, remembering the scene of her superwoman escape. Standing up, she caught the medical doctor's sleeve before he could go. "That's where Dismas is. He's knocked out on the floor. He and John Gonforth tried to kill me with morphine in your office. I—I . . . managed to hit him over the head and break free," she admitted, deciding that was close enough to the truth to make sense. She barely understood the whole magic thing herself and doubted she could explain it to others. "Gonforth admitted to doing anything he could to stop me from keeping him from getting rich. I was to be another victim of an accident."

"That cinches it," Eli exclaimed, turning to Sarah. "We came over here to tell you that the coroner did a second autopsy, and we found that Michael was indeed bludgeoned to death as you suspected. Now we know who did it."

"Jenna, take the doctor back to his office and lock Dismas up in the interrogation room. I'll go after John."

He turned back to Sarah, deep concern in his eyes. "I could put in some calls to the state police and get a few more police officers here if you feel you need protection."

"No, I'm all right," Sarah answered, touched by his

concern and feeling proud she did not twist her left earring. "I just need some time to put everything back in order and to calm down."

"Okay, but keep an ear out for your phone. I'll want you to come down to the station and get your statement once we get your attackers locked up," Eli added, his hand coming up to squeeze her shoulder. "I'm just glad you're safe."

Sarah smiled as the warm feeling of his hand melted into her skin before she reached up to stop him from leaving. The moment her fingers touched his she blushed again, her eyes wide as she struggled to remember what she had wanted to ask. He looked back at her, then smiled and gently pried her fingers from his warm hands. "You'll be okay. We will get all of this taken care of, I promise." He patted her hand before slowly leaving.

Sitting down next to Addie once the others were gone, Sarah smiled, looking down at her fingers that had ever so slightly graced the handsome police chief's hand. Any thoughts of romance faded, however, as Addie rolled over next to her lap, soliciting a good scratch on her belly. Sarah took a deep breath, reached down to oblige Addie, and refocused her mind on the present. She could dream about the future later.

"Addie, I now believe the Leekins are real and you can talk. Now we've just got to make sure we finish what Michael started and stop this development. We've got to save the Leekins and the lynx," she whispered, stroking her companion's fur.

Somehow, saying it aloud to the only animal who could possibly understand made her feel better, if only for a little while.

"*Okay!*" Addie said, as several Leekins hopped out from beneath her thick fur and began to climb up the fabric of the couch. There were about thirty of them this time, and they formed the pyramid just like they did before. They all stared up at Sarah as Clover Figcreek climbed to the very top and gazed into Sarah's eyes with a tentative sort of respect.

Clover Figcreek then took a deep breath and pronounced, "You are a difficult one to understand, Sarah Spellwood. You keep changing things around in the house, you took your time to believe in magic and your witchy powers, and yet you have proved to us that you are our only hope for the survival of our forest home. You finally trusted us and took the potion when your intuition told you to. We are so proud of you."

"Without question," Sarah responded, "I have proven myself to be a formidable advocate; someone with courage and resolve, and with enough of an openness to magic to make good use of the potion you gave me. You protected me just like you protected Michael, and now I am the best person to guard the Leekins and save your home from destruction."

"Thank you, Sarah. If bad people want to hurt you, we will keep you safe. But first, we need to teach you the ways of your ancestor, Lativia Spellwood. Michael told us he wants that. He still speaks in spirit," she added, seeing Sarah's confused expression. "Your actions today have proven you are capable of acting on our behalf. You demonstrated you were worthy of our magical powers, yet you would need further instructions to become the guardian as Michael had been," Clover Figcreek exclaimed, placing her hands on her tiny hips.

Clover Figcreek's skin was pink with joy as she clapped her hands, her tiny wings flickering as she stared at Sarah. "We kept Addie safe while you were gone. We knew that you needed our help. We help you, you help us."

"Thank you all." Sarah smiled, squinting to see the pyramid in front of her bleary eyes. "When those two evil, greedy men tried to kill me, I thought I was a goner."

"That's why we call him the Hunter," Clover Figcreek responded. The other Leekins whimpered and shuddered in fear.

"He sure hunted me. But when I realized what

your potion was capable of, I felt a newfound strength. What was in that potion, anyway?" Sarah inquired.

"That's the power of nature and your namesake, Sarah. You are the descendant of the great witch, Lativia Spellwood of Witchland, and she gave that potion to us." Clover Figcreek smiled, her skin fading back to its dark chocolate color. "The tonic we gave you protects good people who need protecting. No one knows what all its effects are, but it has always kept worthy people safe and ensures they are able to handle whatever problem they face. When you drink this potion, it gives you the powers you need at the moment. It taps into the magic that lies deep inside you, and in the meantime, can make you feel warm and tingly all over!" Clover Figcreek smiled broadly and puffed her chest out.

"Michael would use the potion's power, too, whenever he wanted to help people or when he was in trouble," Addie added with a sad whine, wincing at the thought of Michael no longer being there to help. *"I just wish he had taken the tonic before he was killed."*

Sarah interrupted, "Can you tell me what happened?"

Addie sighed mournfully. *"I was asleep with Michael on his bed when the back door opened, and I woke him. I ran down the stairs to investigate and then that man attacked me. He kicked me hard in the face with his boot and knocked me out. When I awoke, all I saw was Michael lying there, dead."* Addie let out a long, low howl of remorse.

"It's okay, Addie. It's okay," Sarah reassured the whimpering pup. "Which man was it? The huge one or the short one with no hair?"

"The huge one that smells like blood," Addie answered.

"Dismas Lorian." Sarah seethed, her heart starting to hammer with rage and hurt. That man had taken someone very special from her, and she wasn't going to let him get away with it.

"Michael doesn't want revenge," Clover Figcreek spoke up. "He just wants you to protect the forest. And its animals."

"Something else is going on, and it's all about your forest home, Clover Figcreek, although I haven't yet figured out what," Sarah added, moving to lie back down on the couch as she tried not to disrupt the pyramid the Leekins had formed.

Now that the adrenaline had worn off, fatigue crept back into her body.

"What else was going on? Something must have made Dismas kill Michael without John," Sarah mused. "Why else would Dismas kill Michael alone, but John was involved after our meeting? I think John had nothing to do with Michael's death."

"Dismas smelled like blood," Addie barked in answer as she curled up at Sarah's feet. *"Michael didn't like him one bit. He's a hunter."*

Sarah struggled to figure out how Dismas fit into all of this. "He can't be making that much money just for tracking and lying on a lynx survey," she mused.

"I know that Michael was trying to stop him. Michael was always trying to fend for the woods and its animals. He always believed in doing the right thing, even if it meant he would miss out on money," Addie replied. *"One time, he went out in the woods and Michael followed him and stopped him from almost shooting a lynx."*

Sarah's eyes flew wide. "Is Dismas killing the lynx himself? To eradicate them from the forest so that Bert and Morris could pass their environmental impact report?"

"He kills many of them!" Clover Figcreek turned blue and began to sob. "He tracks them and they disappear, never to be seen again. There are so few left in these woods."

Sarah's blood began to boil. "And he felt Michael was a bit too close to home, didn't he? He got so hateful when he heard me mention his report on the lynx populations. That's why he killed Michael, and helped in my attempted murder."

"Yes," Clover Figcreek added, her skin turning

pink again. "Michael was always ready to change the world and make it better. He accepted us whenever we came to him, and we believed in him just as much as he believed in us."

"He was ready to take on big risks and change the world," Sarah agreed, turning onto her side as she closed her eyes. "And now I'm ready, too." Her last words came out in a yawn, punctuated by a deep exhalation as she fell into a deep slumber. Though her blood was boiling over her discovery, she also was completely drained from her ordeal in the doctor's office.

The Leekins collapsed their pyramid, scampered away from the sleeping woman, and rushed back out the door. Addie curled up by Sarah's feet and kept watch over her, not about to let anyone get near the brave and valiant woman she now called her person.

CHAPTER NINETEEN

SARAH WALKED DOWN TO THE POLICE STATION late in the afternoon with her heart pounding in her ears. The few hours' worth of sleep she had managed to snatch did nothing to make her more confident in what she was about to do.

Confronting the men who might have killed Michael, who almost killed her, and didn't seem to have any morals or qualms about killing the forest, was no easy feat.

People gazed at her with curious smiles and stopped to ask if she was okay as she passed them, the news of her heroic escape obviously traveling fast in this small town. Sarah smiled back, her feet automatically taking her around the corner past a small community garden that had been built next to the police station.

"Ah, that's why the flowers in this town are so gorgeous and fragrant." She stopped for a moment to remark on how wonderful the garden was because of the Leekins tending to its care.

Although she felt a bit queasy about the encounter about to ensue, once she passed the garden, she felt a strange warmth like the one she had after taking the potion. She felt her back straighten and her eyes light up as she turned a steely gaze toward the police station.

"I'm Sarah Spellwood, one of the best real estate lawyers in the state and the descendant of Lativia Spellwood. There isn't a living soul here that can stop my power to protect this town and its beloved forest," she told herself.

Sarah's posture became even more upright, her eyes flared, and she marched up to the police station with unequivocal resolve. Her fingers grabbed the door handle and yanked it open with a determined pull.

She marched inside, swallowing hard as she walked from the main entrance into the police station. Jenna was near the back of the front office, standing obediently by the entrance like a sentry. When her eyes caught Sarah's, she smiled and silently guided her through the door which led to the back foyer by the cells. Opening a second door, Jenna led her inside a gray room where a large glass window showed the two men. Her heart quickened when she saw them. Eli paced ominously in front of them, his rage palpable. Occasionally, he spared a glance at the men out of the corner of his eye, causing John Gonforth to shift nervously in his seat.

"We got one of those fancy one-way mirrors from the city after we helped them catch a criminal who was using Witchland as a hideout." Jenna smiled, obviously proud of the little upgrade the humble station had gotten. "Pretty cool, right? They can't see you, but you can see them."

Sarah smiled and nodded at the officer's eagerness, the lighthearted moment briefly interrupting her concentration as she watched the three men on the other side. Based on the beads of sweat on John's and Dismas's foreheads, they'd obviously been in the interrogation room for some time. Meanwhile, Eli looked as menacingly calm as ever. "Yeah, pretty cool," Sarah confessed, a small part of her tickled to see her attackers squirm in fear.

"Officer, you can't keep us here. I know my rights," John growled, his voice becoming desperate as he leaned toward the man. "You have no proof we did anything wrong. You can't hold us here without evidence, and I'm not talking without my attorney present."

"Cut the act, Gonforth," Eli shot back, stopping in his tracks as he slammed his hands down onto the table.

"We've got you red-handed. Sarah told me the whole story."

"It wasn't me," Dismas interjected. "Someone else did it. I was just an innocent victim of a whole conspiracy."

John held up his hand to stop Dismas. "I already told you, not a word!"

"And I suppose the fingerprints we're going to find all over the needle and morphine bottle belong to this 'someone else'?" Eli fired back.

John folded his arms, stoutly refusing to speak. Dismas looked deflated despite his monstrous size.

"Attorney Spellwood already told us that she was the one you captured, she was the one who broke free, and she was the one who launched that plant into your head. That's why you've got blood crusted all over your scalp. We've got witnesses who heard the scuffle at Michael's house, your fingerprints will be all over the morphine bottle, there are rope burns on Sarah's wrists, and there's a wound on Dismas's leg that looks suspiciously like a dog bite, which Sarah told us Addie gave to one of her attackers," Eli continued as he shot a glance at one of the developers.

"I got that while walking in the woods. There was a rabid dog that attacked me—" Dismas started.

"Stop talking," John snarled at Dismas. Then he told Eli, "All circumstantial. None of it proves a thing."

"And yet no one reported you entering or leaving the woods, Dismas, and no one has reported a rabid dog anywhere in the region, and that wound looked pretty fresh when we found you two in the woods. What do you think would happen if we compared the marks of that wound against Addie's teeth?" Eli questioned, expertly navigating their lies and crashing a fist down onto the table. "So, you best get your stories straight. Tell me the truth now, or else you two are going to be arrested for breaking and entering, assault, kidnapping, attempted murder, and the murder of Michael Howler."

"Michael Howler?" John sputtered, clearly confused. "We didn't kill—" Then he froze, realizing he was saying too much. "You can't hold us without allowing me to call my attorney!"

Sarah's lips curled in disdain, recognizing the cruel irony of seeing Michael's adversary—a man who was all about intimidation and blame—being roasted by the facts of his own devious plan. But Sarah could tell his feelings of bewilderment were genuine, and that his protest against Eli's accusation of Michael's murder was real.

"All right, all right, quiet down," Eli shouted, causing John to shut up instantly. "What do you mean you didn't kill Michael?"

John wrung his hands as he wriggled in his seat,

catching his breath as he gathered his thoughts. "I have an alibi for the night Michael was killed, and also for last night." Then he shot Dismas a nasty look. "As do you, I presume, Mr. Lorian?"

"Of course," Dismas stammered, catching on.

"So, if you two have alibis, then who did kill Michael? And who tried to kill Sarah last night?" Eli asked.

"We don't know," John protested. "We just heard he was dead one day."

"Just mysteriously dead from a bludgeoning death, huh?" Eli slammed his fists on the table.

"That's enough," John declared coolly. "We were nowhere near Michael's house when he died, and I have an alibi to prove it. Aren't you going to check up on my alibi? Because if it checks out, you can't hold us any longer."

Outside the window, Sarah turned toward Jenna, thinking hard about what she had heard. "I'm positive his alibis will be false!"

"Were those the two men who attacked you?" Jenna asked, just for confirmation. She watched Sarah nod before she looked back through the window.

Meanwhile, Sarah's fact-based logic was operating at full tilt in her head as she tried to reason how to prove John had murdered Michael.

Dismas and John both provided their alibis. Eli

stalked out of the room, offering Jenna a nod and Sarah a heart-melting smile, before heading into his office to confirm the alibis. A very long time passed, as Sarah waited in suspense, her heart hammering. She prayed that Eli wouldn't have to release the men.

Eli finally returned from the office. Sarah knew from his dejected expression that he had bad news. "Their alibis checked out . . . for now," he said heavily.

"They're false alibis!" Sarah protested desperately. She was terrified of what might happen if the men were released.

Eli placed a calming hand on her shoulder. "Of course, I know that. But I can't hold them. You know that, Sarah."

"You have to investigate those alibis better," she argued.

"I certainly will. I will make sure to nail these guys and get their fingerprints off that morphine bottle. But for now, I have to let them go." Eli sighed. "I'm sorry, Sarah. We'll offer you police protection. I can promise you that."

Sarah narrowed her eyes at the men inside the room. "This is not right at all. I need to warn the Leek —uh—uh . . ." she slipped before catching herself.

Although the Leekins hadn't specifically asked her to keep their existence a secret, their words and actions suggested that not all the folks in town believed in a race of magical faeries living in the surrounding forest. Plus, since she was just learning of their existence herself, she had no idea who was in on the secret.

"You know about the Leekins?" Jenna smiled knowingly. "Huh, I guess it makes sense seeing as how Michael knew about them, and you are his successor. I thought Michael, Hua, Margaret, Eli, and I were the only other ones who knew about them living in our forest. Good to know we can expand the circle."

Sarah nodded. "I've got to warn them *now*."

"Please don't go anywhere without us." Eli sighed. "I'm about to release these two men, and I can't have them on the loose with you unprotected."

But Sarah was already sprinting toward the forest to get to the Leekins.

She used the newfound strength that she had to move through the town as fast as she could. The same people who had seen her pass by before now had looks of confusion on their faces as she rushed past them without saying a word. Oddly enough, as she ran closer to the forest, her energy seemed to increase.

The warmth in her chest blazed into a massive fire as she skidded to a stop in front of the archway to the forest and the mountain. Turning back to look toward her home, Sarah briefly considered going back to get Addie before deciding against it. The faster the Leekins were warned the better, because if she didn't, the lynx's forest home might be destroyed. Images of a dead lynx and felled trees crossed her mind as she rushed across the bridge into the woods.

Just as she began to run up the trails, she heard footsteps behind her. "Sarah, don't!" Eli's deep voice bellowed. "I just released Dismas, and I can't have you getting hurt!"

Sarah paused, as Eli ran up to her. "Just Dismas?"

"John's alibi didn't check out, with some digging. He claimed he was with Bert and Morris last night. They confirmed, but their secretary stated he wasn't there. So we were able to hold him on an attempted murder charge," Eli explained.

Sarah breathed a sigh of relief. "But Dismas is still a problem. I am more worried about him than John, honestly. That's why I have to go warn the Leekins, about what he's doing in the woods."

"I can't let you go around alone," Eli lamented.

"You can't keep me hostage," she reminded him.

"No, but I can at least go with you. We can warn the Leekins together." His earnest look made Sarah feel a bit faint.

"Warn me of what?" A familiar buzzing filled the air and Sarah turned to spot Clover Figcreek hovering in the air beside her ear. Clover Figcreek's wings were a blur as they kept her aloft.

"Dismas is free, and I think he's going to keep killing lynx," Sarah said in a rush.

"Until I can put him away for good," Eli added. Then he paused. "Wait, he's killing lynx? That's a federal poaching offense!"

"It sure is, and he's also getting paid really well by Bert and Morris to ensure there are no lynx left in this forest. He's also selling the lynx for their hides," Sarah explained.

Eli's eyes widened. "You do realize that this is one way to put him away for good, even if we can't indict him on your attempted murder or Michael's murder?"

Sarah slowly grinned. "I was more concerned about saving the lynx, but you're absolutely right. If you can find evidence of him killing lynx or something like that, we can definitely imprison him." Then she twisted her mouth mischievously, a plan forming in her mind. As she told Eli of the plan, he also began to grin.

"You know, I wasn't sure about you at first, with your Beamer and your expensive-looking shoes. My ex-stepfather was a high-rolling attorney in New York, actually, and I have a general distaste for the profession. But you're actually all right." Eli sweetly said, looking into Sarah's eyes admiringly.

Sarah could not hide her blush.

CHAPTER TWENTY

As soon as nightfall washed the town in darkness, Sarah was ready. She put on dark clothes and crept into the woods, letting Addie run ahead of her. Eli met her at the head of the trail and simply nodded at her, letting her know he was prepared. Separating from Eli at the fork in the trail, she deliberately made as much noise as she could as she hiked up the trails toward the hunting preserve and lodge, crunching leaves and twigs under her sensible hiking shoes. *Harriet would approve,* she thought wryly before returning her attention to the dangerous yet thrilling mission at hand.

She ticked off landmarks as she passed them. Everything looked different in the dark, but she was certain she could find her way back. She followed

Addie, whose nose was to the ground searching for Dismas's blood scent.

"We're going to have to go off the path. Don't be scared! Just follow me closely," Addie called when she picked up the scent.

Sarah couldn't help but feel afraid, though, as she stepped into the darkness of the trees. Detritus crunched and squelched under her feet as she attempted to follow Addie's snaking path. She worried Eli might not be able to follow her as he had been. But naturally they couldn't expect Dismas, a seasoned tracker and poacher, to stay on the beaten trail, right?

Sarah followed Addie for what felt like hours. Suddenly, Addie bounded ahead, and Sarah started to run. The top of her foot caught on a knobby tree root protruding sharply from the ground and she tumbled face-first into the ground. It took her a moment to collect her breath, which had been knocked out of her, and scramble back up. "I hope Eli didn't see that face-plant," she whispered with embarrassment, her face already hot and red.

A deep, taunting laughter cut through the sounds of owls, frogs, and night birds as the faint but familiar whimper from a dog was choked off in an instant.

Sarah turned around slowly, feeling watched. She froze when she saw Dismas the Hunter standing behind her, holding a rope that he had cast around

Addie's neck. He held a gun in the other hand, which he was aiming down at Addie as the barrel gleamed in the moonlight streaming into the small clearing he was standing in.

"I didn't think you'd be the one to figure it out, Sarah. Yet, here you are. You're just like Michael, aren't you? Stubborn and persistent to the end." The sneer was audible in his voice, though Sarah couldn't see his face.

"What are you doing out here with that gun? Poaching lynx?" Sarah demanded. In her pocket, she located her recorder and pressed the on button.

"I had a big one in my sights before we heard you crashing through the forest an hour ago. He ran off, and I set my sights on another prey," he replied evilly.

"I can't believe I missed it before," Sarah expressed, trying not to betray her concern for her dog, who looked worried. She didn't like how hard Dismas was pulling up on the rope, cutting off Addie's ability to make any sound. "Even if we can't get you for Michael's murder, we can put you away for good for poaching an endangered species." Sarah stepped forward, no fear at all in her head as the very trees around them seemed to lean closer, all of them intent on what the woman had to say. "You knew that the lynx you wanted so badly was here, but not only was it protected by law, it was also being watched over by the townspeople. But you knew all too well how to sneak by those security cameras. This was all probably a game to you, anyway."

"Hunting is a game," he replied smoothly.

"That's when you came upon an idea. You knew that if the land was sold for development, the townspeople would be too preoccupied with stopping the development to watch the forest very carefully. You just had to align yourself with a couple crooked developers and let them do the dirty work for you. You told them what they needed in terms of an environmental assessment, produced a bogus report for them, claiming there were no lynx present, and satisfied the requirements of the permit. You even got them to write you into the business plan so that you'd make a fortune off of the land deal, while you also made a fortune selling lynx carcasses and hides."

"They make nice blankets and rugs," Dismas snickered. "People want to buy them up, so I'm just cornering a market."

"I must admit that was a stroke of genius on your part—to have them make you a partner in their business. But you're not a land developer. You just like to kill for money. You like to get rich on the pain and blood of others. Michael found out what I know and was going to tell the authorities, so you crept into his house and murdered him before he could talk," Sarah went on boldly, taking another step closer. "All for what, Dismas? A cat that might disappear in twenty or thirty years, anyway? A few million in the bank?" Sarah finished, spreading out her hands and wondering the answer to the question herself. As a good lawyer would, she wanted to understand the facts as well as the motivation behind someone who was willing to bring about the extinction of a species just to satisfy his own personal greed.

The Hunter snarled, his eyes flaring as his lips curled into a scowl. "You've oversimplified things, see. It's not just about the money, though that's pretty nice to have. I've already got fines and jail sentences from those soft-hearted, environmental wimps who want to protect endangered species and deny us hunters the right to take one of the most elusive predators in the country. Sure, it's more about trophies now, but I've adapted to the times, and those endangered-species people haven't. If an animal is endangered, nature takes it out. That's why things go extinct, because they aren't strong enough to survive in today's world. Too bad. It's all about *survival of the fittest*. I'll bet your precious environmental laws don't tell you about that.

"What gives those cagey furballs more rights than us? We're the fit ones, and we're the ones who will outlast 'em. Or do those stupid laws just make you feel the same as those bleeding hearts out there who think humans aren't part of the picture? I'm just helping the process along. That lynx is mine, and no more laws are going to stop me. I have hunted some of the greatest beasts to ever swim, fly, or crawl across the earth. Every hunt is legitimate to me, not to mention a great test of skill and prowess. It is the ultimate man-versus-nature challenge, and that lynx is going to be the last head on my trophy wall before I retire from these woods."

Sarah stepped back as the Hunter cackled and advanced toward her. "Just like an animal, you understand the power of the gun. Namely, whoever holds it, holds the power. Michael got proof of what I was doing and tried to get in my way, and with those stuffed shirts from the government breathing down my neck, I had to take him out quickly before he talked. Thankfully, I didn't even have to use a gun. Michael obliged by letting me wrestle that stupid cane out of his hands and knock him down the stairs, making it look like an accident all on his own.

"Then all I had to do was encourage those bumbling idiots to cut me into the deal. I would get them all arrested or have them 'disappear' and then claim my four hundred acres and the Witchland Forest land as my own personal hunting ground. Buying out Oscar's hunting lodge, too. I'll still raze some of the land, put in some hotels, and build up a nice little money-maker for my retirement, but I seriously doubt anyone will care about a dumb little wildcat once they see how much havoc this development is going to wreak," Dismas finished.

"What are you going to do? Shoot me?" Sarah fired back. "Do you really think you'll get away with a second murder? Eli's been notified, and he's on his way, bringing several state police and federal government agents with him," Sarah bluffed, feeling her power flare up in her as she leaned forward. Hopefully, that would buy her a little more time.

Dismas dropped Addie's makeshift leash before placing a foot on it and holstering his gun. The holstering was fast, almost too fast to see, and the message was clear. The Hunter knew how to use his weapon.

"They'll be too busy recovering the pieces of your body." He chuckled, reaching into his pocket to pull out a chunk of dead animal meat, stuffing something inside of it, and tossing it onto the ground in front of Addie's muzzle. Addie began to sniff at it curiously, her mouth salivating, even though she knew what was going on.

"That herb I just filled that meat with will send your cute little animal into a bloodthirsty rage. The second Addie eats that meat, she'll tear you to shreds, and then I will kindly put her out of her misery so you can be found dead together. They'll just think she was another rabid dog. There's been one in these woods lately, who bit me." He snickered. "Now eat up, little doggie." He pointed to the meat as Addie began to back away from it.

"Eat it, you dumb dog," he growled, pushing her toward the meat with his boot. "Go on. Eat it. Now," he ordered, groaning as Addie turned her nose away.

Intelligence the Hunter could not detect sparkled behind Addie's eyes. She knew everything that was going on, as tempting as the raw meat smelled to her.

Sarah held her breath as Addie refused to follow the order, thinking it was no wonder Dismas killed animals—he couldn't even understand them. When the Hunter's eyes flashed up to look at her, Sarah set her famous green-eyed stare right back at him.

Addie snarled in anger as Dismas drew his knife and gun, holding both in a combat stance as he advanced toward Sarah. "Fine. If the dog won't do it, I'll just kill you both the easy way."

"Aieeeeeeeee!"

A ferocious scream filled the air as both Sarah and the Hunter looked around, momentarily stunned by the wailing. Addie's ears perked up, and several footsteps could be heard approaching. In the next instant, a huge tree limb cracked right above the Hunter's head and smashed down upon his back, knocking him and the gun to the ground. He bellowed in pain and shock.

"Freeze!" Eli shouted, running up and aiming his gun down at the Hunter as Jenna rushed over and kicked the man's weapons aside. A horde of angry Leekins followed, shooting through the air on their wings in a formation that allowed them to collectively carry several pine cones. They began to furiously pelt the man with the cones, while shouting and cursing in a garbled-sounding Leekin tongue. When Dismas fainted, they landed on the ground and rapidly formed a pyramid beneath Sarah as Clover Figcreek let out a piercing screech that made Sarah's hair stand on end.

"Aieeeeeeee! We heard you and Addie were in trouble, so we came to save you from the Hunter." The Leekin stretched her arms out with a huge smile of triumph. "It's been a long time since we've gotten to throw pine cones at people! It is loads of fun!" she added, with the other Leekins cheering in agreement.

"*That was* outstanding, *Clover Figcreek*," Addie barked.

With complete confidence, Addie walked toward the Hunter, growling.

"Why, you dirty little mutt . . ." Dismas snarled, coming to.

"Don't even try to get up, Dismas. It's over," Eli answered, pushing the pile of pine cones off of Dismas and handcuffing the Hunter while keeping his boot on the man's back to keep him still. "Jenna, radio back to the station and tell the other officers to wait for us there. We've got things under control here."

As Jenna moved off to radio in, Eli stepped over to Sarah. The Leekins swarmed all over Dismas, continuing to pelt him with pine cones. Eli leaned down to pet Addie before he gave Sarah a warm smile that made her heart skip a few beats. "Nice job solving the mystery, Sarah."

"I even got his confession on recording," she crowed proudly.

"Excellent! What an idiot, confessing everything like that. Now we've got all the proof we need to lock him up for good with your recording. Once the Leekins get done with him, we'll send him and the others to the city for arraignment and sentencing in court," Eli declared. "Should be open and shut."

"Good, but what do you mean 'when the Leekins get done with him'? Is there something I should know?" Sarah asked, turning toward the creatures who were swarming over Dismas like ants.

"See for yourself," Eli answered, tossing the Leekins a smile as Clover Figcreek began ordering her troop around the man's body. "Wow, Dismas is beginning to look more and more like a blue mummy, grimacing in pain whenever he tries to move." Sarah giggled. "What's that?" She peered at the rope the

Leekins began to use to reinforce his handcuffs. It didn't look like any twine she had seen before.

"It's rope drenched with magic," Eli started, noticing Addie wincing as he patted her head with a sheepish glance. "Sorry, girl, but you're safe; he can't get to you now," he added before he continued. "Basically, if Dismas moves or struggles, the rope tightens. It is also made with a sedating spell, which will keep him nice and calm until we can move him to the station. It is a surprisingly effective tool for keeping people still, which is why the Leekins use it for special occasions. It's one of their weapons that they whip up when branches and pine cones alone won't do."

"It won't kill him, though, right?" Sarah asked, wringing her hands nervously. Even a murderer like Dismas doesn't deserve that fate, and Michael wouldn't want that anyway.

"Of course not," Clover Figcreek sputtered indignantly. "We can't kill things. Our job is to give and protect life. After we tighten the rope a few times, we're going to give him a potion to make him forget about us Leekins and the lynx so he will never threaten us again!"

Then the head Leekin whistled, and several more of her kind emerged from the darkness of the trees. Together, they carried a similar vial to the one they had given Sarah. The liquid inside glowed, lighting their path.

With one heave, they hoisted the vial over Dismas's face and tipped it down the man's throat while the Hunter remained completely docile throughout the process. Dismas's skin glowed with a golden light as the vial's contents took effect, and then the Leekins began to scatter again, vanishing into the leaves and underbrush of their home without another word.

"What's that for?" Sarah inquired. These creatures were both puzzling and mesmerizing to watch.

"It will make him a good man and remove all of his desire to kill ever again," Clover Figcreek answered.

"Why didn't you just use that in the first place?" Eli asked, genuinely curious. Sarah felt relieved to learn that Eli did not know everything about these mysterious beings, either.

"Well, we tried, and he wouldn't let us come near him," Clover Figcreek replied in an annoyed tone, as if the answer should have been perfectly obvious.

"He was pretty scary," Sarah acknowledged.

"He couldn't see us, but he thought we were gnats. He was always swatting at us," another Leekin piped up in a shrill voice.

Sarah peered down at him, surprised to hear how the other Leekins sounded compared to their leader, who had a much more commanding voice. It was an endearing voice, really.

Dismas began to snore, a deep rumbling growl from the depths of his throat. Such a snore was befitting for the big man, who was now more like a gentle beast.

"Thank you for helping us, Sarah." Clover Figcreek smiled, alighting onto Addie's head and reaching out for a handshake. "Now our forest is safe, and I know Michael would be proud of you for all you have done for us and the humans that live in Witchland. Know that we owe you a great debt of gratitude and that you will forever have our help, should you need it, as well as the power of our magic on your side."

"You're welcome, Clover Figcreek," Sarah responded, offering her pinky tip to shake the little creature's hand. When Clover Figcreek touched her, she felt a warm tingle in her skin that spread gently up her arm.

"I'll keep helping you no matter what happens because you, this forest, and Michael's legacy need to be honored and protected. Who knows, maybe one day I'll actually get used to all this magic stuff and understand it as well as Michael did," Sarah went on.

The Leekin leader turned a fierce pink and giggled. "Thank you, Sarah. We're glad to have you as a friend to the forest." She flew up and then paused, adding over her shoulder, "Even if you mess up Michael's home and have spunk." Then she fluttered off into the darkness, followed by her fellow Leekins, and the forest became still.

Eli patted Sarah's shoulder and smiled. "Good to know; we can always use some more good folks in this town. I'm headed back to the station."

As he grabbed Dismas by the arms and wrangled him up with Jenna's assistance, the ropes attached to him slithered off, and then they dissolved the moment they touched the earth. "I can only imagine that if Michael was watching, he'd be very proud of you," Eli told Sarah, before marching his dazed quarry out of the clearing and out of sight.

Sarah failed to hide yet another blush as she began to trudge after the police chief and his deputy. Eli may not have realized it, but he had just given her the most meaningful praise he could have.

Addie stared up at her with a dangling tongue, rooing softly, *"You like him, don't you? You like the police chief."*

"No . . . I . . . well—er—" Sarah said, blushing even redder as the snickering giggles of a couple hundred Leekins filled the air behind her. She had thought the Leekins had already gone away to their home by the old fence.

"You do. I think he likes you, too," Addie barked, her tail wagging as Sarah's eyes widened.

"Really?" Sarah asked. "You think so?"

"*Yep,*" Addie answered, causing Sarah to feel a new warmth inside her. If Eli liked her back, that changed a few things.

As Sarah Spellwood walked back to her home, deep in conversation with her dog, she smiled to herself. All the things she didn't believe in—those mythical beings, her witch ancestor Lativia, and her talking dog—all had helped her through the adventure she had been through, and none of it seemed so fantastical anymore.

In fact, it was beginning to seem more normal than ever before. "Besides," she said with a sigh, "while living in this town, it might be a good thing to have a little crush to keep things interesting. Though after this sort of introduction to Witchland, I can't imagine it ever being boring here."

CHAPTER TWENTY-ONE

"Well, Michael, you chose a good spot to lay down roots and live out the rest of your life." Sarah sighed, sitting with Addie on a bench in front of a gravestone that read 'Michael Howler' in big engraved letters.

She had helped Margaret and Hua scatter Michael's ashes in the forest right by the Leekins' fence, which he had loved. The entire town had pitched in for a lovely gravestone, which was now covered in an ever-growing offering of flowers and trinkets from both townsfolk and the Leekins, who were all eager to show their respect for their hero.

Sarah had been coming to speak to her mentor at least twice a week, speaking about town life, cases she was working on, and how her days had been. Addie would often come along and regale her former owner with tales of dog life, such as how she had found a bone buried in the yard, or the ever-so-exciting tale of how she had chased a dancing ball around the room. Addie swore up and down that Michael visited them often and watched over them, but Sarah had not seen or heard him, so she felt close to him by sitting next to his memorial.

"I'm just glad you passed this metaphorical torch on to me and that I can help people the same way you did," Sarah shared. "Thank you for sending me that letter and giving me a new lease on life. I feel much happier here than I ever did in the city.

"Bert and Morris failed the environmental impact assessment and are gone. John and Dismas are both serving time for the crimes they committed. We finally got justice for your death, Michael, though that still doesn't bring you back. I miss you every day, but at least you can rest in peace, knowing that the Leekins are also safe, as are the creatures that they protect. And Witchland is never going to be changed into an obscene tourist trap, at least not as long as I am here.

"Addie and I are trying to keep things safe out here, while Harriet makes fun of my wardrobe choices," she added, joking a bit. "I don't have much demand for real estate cases, so I've been taking on whatever cases people here need. I have also started studying magic, animal telepathy, and environmental law—trying to fill your massive shoes in my own way." Sarah glanced down at her tennis shoes, smiling softly to herself. Both physically and metaphorically, Michael had far bigger shoes than she could ever hope to fill, but she would try. She also couldn't believe that she had sold her Jimmy Choos on eBay and had started wearing comfortable tennis shoes or hiking shoes, with only one pair of really nice heels left in her closet for court appearances.

"Clover Figcreek and the Leekins need someone to make their world better, and it looks like right now I'm the best candidate for the job." Sarah paused for a moment, unsure of what else to say until Addie looked up.

"Tell him about Eli," Addie barked, wagging her tail.

"He doesn't want to hear about Eli," Sarah chided as Addie tilted her head to the side.

"How do you know? He's listened to everything else you've said without complaint."

"Fine," Sarah conceded, turning back to the gravestone with a conciliatory look on her face, as if Michael's spirit would come out and judge her for having a crush on the police chief.

"He doesn't even know I like him yet, but it's getting to be a good friendship that I cherish. Once I get up the courage, I'll let him know how I feel. Who knows, maybe we'll even start to date. And I stopped that stupid habit of twisting my left earring!" She shrugged, trying to act casual about her burning feelings.

Sarah closed her mouth and stroked Addie's fur, unsure what else she could say about how things were going before she said her goodbyes and stood up and walked back through the forest. Having Michael close by kept any thoughts about missing him away, especially with the Leekins taking such good care of his memorial.

As she found her way onto the trail again, Addie suddenly froze and raised her hackles, staring into the trees. "What is it, girl?" Sarah froze as well, trusting Addie's instincts.

"*A lynx!*" Addie barked and jumped up in excitement.

Something rustled through the brush. Then a beautiful gray-and-black cat emerged, the white tufts of hair sprouting from its ears adding to the cute pointedness of its face. It paused on the edge of the trail, and Sarah expected it to either run off or back away from Addie slowly. When it continued to stand there, staring directly at them both, Sarah began to feel the hairs raise on her neck.

"*Thank you,*" she heard, clear as day. The voice

was honey smooth and strangely sexless, hinting at great power and grace beneath its serene intonation.

"Are you talking to me?" Sarah mumbled. Though she had gotten used to talking with Addie, other animals had not yet spoken to her like humans. She still briefly wondered at times if she really had lost her mind and none of this was real, or if the Leekin potion really had worked to bring out the powers she had suppressed. This seemed to be living proof of the latter.

"*I am Susu, and I was the lynx Dismas was about to kill when you confronted him in the woods,*" the lynx went on smoothly. "*I must thank you.*"

Sarah gulped. "You're welcome," she managed, her sense of being stunned audible in her tone.

"*You have proved to have the bravery of a lion and the heart of a tiger,*" Susu complimented. "*Therefore, I wish to offer you the bravery, strength, and grace of myself and my kind. The lynx is now your spirit animal guide; you can turn to the lynx when you require bravery, strength, or grace in your endeavors to protect this forest. We now align ourselves with you and will always come to your aid if you need us.*"

"That—that is quite an honor." Sarah nodded. She made a mental note that she needed to look into animal spirit guides, as she had no idea what they were.

Susu seemed to read her thoughts. "*Animal spirit*

guides will come to you in dreams or in real life to give you wisdom and insight you need. We lend you our strengths and traits. We also protect you; if someone were to try to hurt you, one of us will leap to your defense. We are friends, until the day you die," she explained.

Addie let out a little whine, salivating. Though she was a good dog and knew to hang back, her instincts were going into overdrive, telling her to chase the slinky gray cat before her. Sarah put a staying hand on her head and thanked the lynx again.

Susu shot Addie a dirty look before letting out a purr and then turning back into the forest. She didn't even make a sound as she disappeared into the thick brambles.

Sarah felt spellbound for a moment. "So many crazy yet wonderful things happen here," she muttered to herself, before praising Addie for being so obedient. The honor of what had just transpired hit her as she returned home, her heart beating in her chest.

Exiting the forest like she always did, she made her way back home, her head filled with confidence and held high as she walked through the town. The warmth she had been feeling for several days hadn't left her yet and, in fact, only seemed to be changing in intensity as she moved on with her life.

"Sarah! Sarah!" Hua called, waving her over

toward the greenhouse before giving her a tight hug. Margaret came out of the greenhouse and joined in the embrace, both women giddy with excitement.

"I know we already congratulated you a gazillion times, but we want to thank you *again* for all you have done for the town. What would we have done without you?" Margaret added. "You've certainly earned our respect and gratitude, as well as the respect of the people of this town. Michael managed to touch a lot of people during his time here, and it seems like you have followed in his footsteps perfectly."

"You certainly seem a lot more confident. Please come in while we water some plants," Hua said, pulling Sarah back into the greenhouse and shutting the door before they both bent down to pet Addie. "Maybe we can help you learn a thing or two about the history of this little town and who you really are."

Sarah raised her eyebrows at the remarks, unsure what she could be taught about her past. Sure, she knew about her magical origins, especially now as she was getting more accustomed to the magical ways of the Leekins, but how that played into her current role as Michael's successor seemed unclear.

"How so?" Sarah asked, tugging at her collar a bit to try to cool off. The summer was taking hold, making the air sticky in the afternoons. The humidity of the greenhouse and the heady manure smell made the heat a thousand times more insufferable.

Hua spoke first. "Before we tell you more, we have to solve one mystery for you of how Addie got to your door in New York. It was Margaret and I who brought Addie to you. Michael instructed us to do so if anything happened to him because he knew we lived in Manhattan many years ago. Our job was to deliver Addie and the envelope we left on your door. We waited for you out of sight, as per Michael's instructions. When we saw you come down the street, we headed back to Witchland. We knew Addie was safe once you arrived. We also slipped that note under your door because we knew from the beginning that Michael was murdered, and we knew it was by John Gonforth. No one believed us; they all still think we are eccentric New Yorkers. We needed someone else to look into it, to take it seriously, and we knew you would because you loved Michael so. We knew you could help Officer Eli turn his doubts about the case into real suspicions."

"That explains a lot." Sarah nodded.

"Now, we mentioned before we were witches, and you seemed skeptical. Are you still skeptical?" Margaret asked.

"No—well, er, um . . ." Sarah trailed off, uncertain how to answer that. Of course she believed in magic now, but what would it mean if she admitted that to these women? She realized she still had an ounce of skepticism, as well as a lingering concern about her mental health.

"Do me a favor and look at that flower over there," Margaret instructed, pointing to a stem sitting in its own little trough of dirt.

The label beside it said it was sage, and it looked like it had just been planted a few weeks prior. It was a little green shoot and wasn't in flower by any means, but Sarah looked at it anyway without any questions. Then she gasped as the tiny stem leaned forward, just like the potted plant had done when she was tied up in the doctor's office. The urge to ask the plant to do something filled her, as strong as it had been in the office a few months earlier. The urge moved up her throat, almost agonizingly so, as the words tried to form in her mouth and break past her shocked lips. *The stem of that plant certainly couldn't move like that,* she thought, *and there wasn't any wind to make it move in the confined greenhouse.*

"Tell it to grow," Hua whispered with excitement, her voice quivering a bit.

"Grow," she kindly requested, and she watched the plant sprout more leaves and shoot upward as if it was in a time-lapse movie, growing a thicker stem with beautiful, tiny purple flowers. Within five seconds, it was a fully grown sage plant.

"H—how? How did I—"

Margaret smiled and wordlessly flicked her hand at a crop of tomato plants, upon which the green fruit that were hanging motionlessly from it before all of a sudden began to swell. Their color shifted from green to yellow to juicy red. Soon, the fully mature fruits rested comfortably on the dirt, tugging the stems of the plants down with their weight, as if they had been that way all along.

Hua chuckled and waved her hand, causing the watering can to rise up off the floor and bob over all the plants, watering them precisely before floating back down to the table.

Then both women turned to look at Sarah's shocked face, before gently reaching over to clasp her shoulders. "Don't worry, you have this power of the forest as well, and now that the Leekins have unlocked it for you, we will help you learn how to use it." Margaret smiled.

"Is that—is that why that plant sacrificed itself for me?" Sarah stammered. "Because I'm some kind of forest witch?"

"Indeed," Margaret said.

"I feel so bad about that." Sadness welled in her

heart for the dead plant. She wished she would have repotted it.

Hua laid a hand on her forearm and said kindly, "Don't worry, we went into the office the next day to check on the plant, and the doctor had repotted it. We gave it some fresh soil and water, and it will be fine."

Sarah breathed a sigh of relief. "That's good news!"

"You're becoming a great witch now, Sarah, and you've got quite the journey ahead of you," Hua added. "Come in, let's get some soup, and then we'll talk about how Margaret and I discovered our power as herbal witches."

Sarah could only nod, knowing that what she had seen was seemingly impossible. These women appeared to be suggesting that they were going to be her teachers, to help her believe that the impossible was often quite possible . . . and true. In her mind, she found herself wanting to leave, to go back home to her couch and curl up with her mystery novel. This was all too crazy and bizarre, a million miles outside of her comfort zone.

Instead, she channeled the bravery of the lynx and followed the women into their home, anxious to see what these unlocked powers of hers could do.

"Now, the day I heard a plant first talk to me, I thought I was insane," Margaret began, ladling soup into a bowl for Sarah while Hua fussed with a teapot.

"I had been having dreams—well, I thought they were dreams—of these little brown faeries visiting me at night."

"Leekins? In the city?" Sarah asked.

"Not Leekins; brownies. Similar, but not the same. There are countless faery species all over the world. Anyway. These brownies were taking care of the herbs I had started growing in my fire escape, just for the scent, you know. But they opened an entire world to me. They led me to her." Margaret pointed at Hua.

"I am a first generation Vietnamese American," Hua explained proudly. "I was living in Chinatown with my aunt's family in a crowded apartment, working in an organic grocery co-op and growing plants on their rooftop garden. I was a farmer's daughter in Vietnam, you see, and my father taught me herbal magic. I had been doing it since I was a little girl, as it came naturally to everyone in my family. In New York, I was called the plant whisperer and no one knew about my magical abilities; they just saw the results. I could work miracles with plants, even bringing back ones that seemed to be beyond saving. The co-op loved me and referred people to me who needed help with their plants. Margaret came to me one day, needing help, because her parsley had developed mildew, and that's how it all started."

"Those brownies wouldn't leave me alone about

that mildew." Margaret rolled her eyes. "They would wake me up constantly. Then one day, I dreamed—or rather, thought I dreamed—that I drank some potion they made me, and in the morning, I heard the parsley tell me to go to this co-op down the street for advice." She laughed. "I thought I had gone out of my mind, but that plant was essentially handing me my destiny. I couldn't believe how my life changed over the next year, how much happier I was, and how I managed to survive so long without plants and life all around me before that."

Hua slid her arm around Margaret's waist. "We found each other, and life just became magical after that. We grew as witches and developed each other's natural powers. Then we found our way here, where Daisy taught us what we didn't already know about magic and herbalism."

Margaret beamed down at Hua before planting a tender kiss on her forehead. "It's been such a journey, but we have become our true selves here in this town."

"Sounds a bit like my story," Sarah admitted. "I always talked to a goat and plants and things when I was a kid, especially when I visited Aunt Beth's farm here, but I thought that was just me being an imaginative little kid. When I first heard Addie talking and met the Leekins a few months ago, I thought I was losing my mind!"

"Far from it. You're just growing into who you were meant to be, unlocking precious ancestral gifts that it would be a shame to waste," Margaret explained.

Despite wanting to go home and read about some other mystery in some novel, it seemed like Sarah's next mystery was about to unfold right before her eyes in her real life.

**Curious about how Sarah and Addie solve their next mystery?
Get Howl Play Now!**

http://getbook.at/howlplay

A NOTE FROM MELANIE

Ms. Addie Pants who inspired this series and loves to tear her toys to shreds!

Thanks so much for reading this book. I love hanging out with Sarah and Addie as well as the other characters in this book. Not only did they keep me busy but we all become good friends—except for the bad guys.

Being an author is an awesome profession and I feel blessed to be able to finally live my passion.

Stay tuned for a sneak preview of the second book in the series, *Howl Play*, which is now available on Amazon.

Click here to skip the preview and read the whole magical book. https://getbook.at/howlplay. Thanks again!

    With Beautiful Magic,
    Melanie Snow and Addie

PS: Reviews help authors keep writing. Please feel free to leave one!

But despite hours of study and her talking dog's support, she still doubts her spellcasting skill. And she's about to face a major test when she's plunged into a battle between good and evil after the enchanted forest's protective deed is stolen and the town clerk brutally murdered...

With the finger pointing at woodland wolves for the fatal mauling, Sarah and her pooch pal vow to help the handsome police officer Eli Strongheart dig up the truth and clear the innocent creatures' names. But when darkness rises to threaten the unprotected woods and its inhabitants, she'll need to fight a formidable magical enemy to stop its destruction.

Can Sarah save the wolves and recover the deed before Witchland meets a terrible fate?

Howl Play is the second book in the sweet Spellwood Witches paranormal cozy mystery series. If you like cute flirty romance, discovering one's true destiny, and love for animals, then you'll adore Melanie Snow's barking-ly fun adventure.

Buy *Howl Play* to let supernatural talent off the leash today!
https://getbook.at/howlplay

Do you want to know what happens to Sarah and Addie now as they continue on their quest? Or what about Michael Howler: what is his magical journey? You will be able to find out in the next book of the series: Howl Play!

Howl Play is now available on Amazon. Download your copy right now! https://getbook.at/howlplay

Not ready to get your own copy? Enjoy part of the first chapter for free on the next page!

Howl Play

Chapter 1 . . . in part

Howl Play, Book 2 of The Spellwood Witches

Sarah opened her eyes. The first ray of sun pushed through the bedroom curtains, adding a tinge of warmth to the cold gray of the tiny upstairs room. In her fuzzy pajamas, underneath the thick quilt and flannel comforter, she could only feel the morning chill on her nose and cheeks.

Sarah smiled as she realized she thought of this little room and bed as hers. It had been several months since her entanglement with the nasty real estate developers and Dismas Lorian. Already she had fallen into a rhythm, a routine of comfort and harmony. She had even started to sleep upstairs in Michael's old bed again, having solved her former mentor's murder and apprehended Dismas the Hunter, a hired environmental surveyor with his own personal vendetta to eliminate endangered lynx from the woods, who had killed Michael when he had gotten in the way. Solving the murder had helped her vanquish her fear of the stairs on which Michael had died. Every corner and curve of Michael's house was becoming familiar to her, as if she had always lived here. Her life as an over-worked New York City attorney squished into a tiny office and an even tinier apartment, scurrying for taxis or fighting crowds in the subway—it now all felt like a dream, like something that had never truly happened to her.

Addie stretched alongside Sarah; her ears flopped across the quilt adorably. Even in sleep, it was now obvious that she was no ordinary dog; there was some-thing far too human, too sharp, in the expression on her sleeping face. She bolted upright, a split second before the sound of a knock.

"Margaret's here," Addie remarked.

Sarah cracked a grin. Already she was able to understand Addie without the Leekins—those pesky little faeries who finally became allies when they helped Sarah save Witchland. Sarah loved the long conversations and running narratives of her little life shared with Addie in Michael's cottage. Sarah was also starting to be able to talk to plants on her own. As a novice witch, she found delight in balancing her magical studies with her legal career and her new forays into environmental law. Though law and magic seemed to be polar opposites, Sarah was melding them together to achieve her passion, preserving the Witchland Forest.

"Rise and shine!" Margaret hollered shrilly.

One thing Sarah had not yet grown accustomed to was how her neighbors—and, indeed, most people in Witchland—rose at the very crack of dawn. They had so much energy without even a sip of coffee!

"Hi," she said wanly, pushing the door open.

"You ready?" Margaret chirped, all energy and smiles.

"I thought we might do it a bit later in the day." Sarah shifted, feeling the comfy bed upstairs calling to her still.

"No! This is the best time for potion-making! When the plants are happiest, the most eager to give." She took Sarah's hand and started to pull her to their cottage next door.

"Hang on! I need to get dressed!" Sarah protested.

Margaret glanced down at Sarah's fuzzy fleece pajamas with their little clouds and sheep. "Oh. Right. Well, hurry! We have a lot of work to do!"

Sarah pulled on some clothes in a hurry. Then she met Margaret out front and followed her to the neighboring cottage. Addie trotted along behind them.

"This is going to be fun, Sarah. And don't worry, I'm here to give you moral support," yipped Addie.

Sarah always felt enveloped in warmth and love whenever she entered Margaret and Hua's humble cottage. There were plants everywhere—beans sprouting on the table, herbs growing on windowsills, exotic vines covered with an abundance of fragrant, jewel-like flowers snaking across the backs of chairs and up the walls, a greenhouse behind the main house that was so densely packed with plants of all varieties that it was almost hard to breathe inside its jungle-like fragrance and humidity. Their house and greenhouse felt like perpetual summer, while their garden had embraced autumn, with colorful squashes and pump-kins swelling at the end of verdant vines. The sense of abundant life and joy suffused the entire property, adding the vibrations of so many little plant spirits to mingle with their own.

"Good morning!" Hua breezed into the kitchen, her colorful kimono swirling around her slim frame and her face full of energy and pep. "Hi, cute puppy!" She beamed and pecked Sarah on the cheek and gave Addie a kiss on her nose. "Are you sure you're ready?"

"Well, I'm still half asleep," Sarah admitted sheep-ishly. "But I've been dying for our first lesson. I've been putting it off because, well, I've been incredibly busy with studying." The memory of long nights buried in environmental law books and paranormal books gave her a headache just thinking back on them.

Hua waved her excuse away, but Margaret peered at her, clearly unconvinced. Sarah did not like how Margaret searched her face, seeming to read things that lay under the surface of her smile. Both women were eerily perceptive, but Margaret tended to give Sarah chills with her intuition.

"Do you have any injuries?" Hua asked first.

"Um?" Sarah began searching her body. Finally, with Addie's help, she located a tiny bruise on her ankle. She was in awe of her dog, who could sniff out anything with her nose. In fact, it was Addie's nose that helped her locate Dismas, the Hunter, in the dark woods at night and, thus, solve the lynx case and Michael's murder.

"Perfect! Now watch that bruise and take a sip of this." Hua thrust a tureen toward Sarah. "It is best to instruct the plants in the potion to do what you want, by the way," she added.

The potion tasted like warm carrot ginger soup. As its tingle spread down her throat to her stomach, Sarah instructed the plants to help heal her. Before her very eyes, Sarah watched the purple of the bruise fade and finally vanish into the milk white of her inner ankle. A tiny freckle on her ankle now stood out, chestnut once again. She gasped. "Wow! This stuff really works!"

"It is one of the simplest recipes and incantations you can learn—but it works. It is still magic, herbal magic. This is our first lesson today." Hua began to teach Sarah the various components of the potion and how to speak to the plants and prepare them.

GET YOUR COPY NOW
https://getbook.at/howlplay

DISCOVER
THE SPELLWOOD WITCHES SERIES

———

WITCH'S TAIL, BOOK 1

Can she awaken her dormant powers and stop a desperate killer destroying the forest? If you like paranormal puzzles, delightful canine companions, and environmental enlightenment, then you'll love Melanie Snow's wagging-ly fun whodunit.

Here's the link to buy the book today!
http://getbook.at/witchstail

FISH AND BLAME, FREE NOVELLA

Can Sarah embrace her newly discovered magical powers? Will she and her hound familiar find the troubled murderer in time? If you like engaging whodunits, then you'll love Melaine Snow's fun novella.

Here's the link to get your free novella today!
https://wendyvandepoll.com/
melaniesnowfishandblame

HOWL PLAY, BOOK 2

A novice witch. A collie companion. Can this clever duo put noses to the ground to chase down a killer? If you like cute flirty romance, discovering one's true destiny, and love for animals, then you'll adore Melanie Snow's barking-ly fun adventure.

Here's the link to buy the book today!
   http://getbook.at/howlplay

TAIL OF A FEATHER, BOOK 3

A mysterious portal. Eight crows with a message. A missing police chief. If you like paranormal puzzles, charming canine companions, and a bit of flirty romance, then you will love Melanie Snow's crafty quest. Take flight into the magical world of Witchland.

Here's the link to buy the book today!
   http://getbook.at/tailofafeather

IMPAWSIBLE MISCHIEF, BOOK 4

Stolen charms. A mysterious woman running for mayor. Can beginner's magic save an ill-fated land? If you like wisecracking creatures, enchanting characters, and close-knit sisterhoods, then you'll love Melanie Snow's clever story.

Here's the link to buy the book today!
http://getbook.at/impawsiblemischief

PAWTRAYAL, BOOK 5

When a ghost cries murder, an unsolved case could cost her future. Can this witch solve the magical mystery when an old enemy starts casting chaos. If you like wise familiars, heartthrob romances, and mystical whodunits, then you'll love Melanie Snow's paranormal brainteaser.

Here's the link to buy the book today!
http://getbook.at/pawtrayal

Don't Miss Your Free Gift!

Thank you for purchasing Witch's Tail, The
Spellwood Witches, Book 1

Here is the link to get your Free
Novella Now

https://wendyvandepoll.com/melaniesnowfishandblame

About Melanie Snow

Melanie Snow is the pen name for Wendy Van de Poll, a bestselling author, pet loss grief coach, and animal medium. She is the author of The Spellwood Witches, a paranormal cozy mystery series.

Her books weave together positive magic, snarky forest faeries, and insightful animals with fun and eclectic humor. True life adventures and intuition are woven into her stories laced with unbridled imagination.

She has been followed by wild wolves in minus sixty degrees, hissed at by a mama bobcat, and played ball with a wild owl—among other animal encounters.

Find out more about her work by visiting her at https://wendyvandepoll.com/melanie-snow.

And also get *Fish and Blame*
A Free Novella

Download Your Free Gift
https://wendyvandepoll.com/melaniesnowfishandblame

HOW TO FIND MELANIE SNOW

www.wendyvandepoll.com/melanie-snow

www.facebook.com/melaniesnow.cozymysteries

www.instagram.com/melaniesnow.cozymysteries

www.facebook.com/groups/melaniesnowcozymysteries

www.amazon.com/author/melaniesnow

www.goodreads.com/melaniesnowcozymysteries

A Free Novella ~ *Fish and Blame*

https://wendyvandepoll.com/
melaniesnowfishandblame

ACKNOWLEDGMENTS

I would like to thank my intuitive writing team who has guided me to write this fun series. They weren't always easy to deal with but they were patient with my fumbling. Because of them Melanie Snow and all the characters in my head have come to life.

I appreciate all my teachers of the furred, feathered, and finned variety who continue to guide me through life and teach me what matters.

A special thanks goes to my weekly writing buddies H.R. Hobbs and Toni Crowe who are kind, sassy, and amazing authors.

I offer a tremendous amount of appreciation to my beta readers: Nadine, Vicky, and Renee. To my editor

Robyn Margaret Verdugo a huge thank you for your expertise. And thank you to my talented proofreader Allison Rose.

A huge hug goes to my husband, Rick Van de Poll. He is a remarkable poet and human being who dedicates his life to the animals and the environment. He inspires my soul. You can find his books on Amazon, as well.

And of course, Addie. This rescue puppy flew on a jet plane from Texas to grace my life in many ways and writing books with her as a main character is just one. Addie even has her own series called; The Adventures of Ms. Addie Pants on Amazon.